MW00438925

Cake

Johns Hopkins: Poetry and Fiction
John T. Irwin, General Editor

Stories by
Tristan Davies

The Johns Hopkins University Press

Baltimore and London

This book has been brought to publication with the generous
assistance of the G. Harry Pouder Fund.

© 2003 The Johns Hopkins University Press
All rights reserved. Published 2003
Printed in the United States of America on acid-free paper

9 8 7 6 5 4 3 2 1

The Johns Hopkins University Press
2715 North Charles Street
Baltimore, Maryland 21218-4363
www.press.jhu.edu

Library of Congress Cataloging-in-Publication Data

Davies, Tristan, 1963–
Cake: stories / by Tristan Davies.
       p.   cm.—(Johns Hopkins, poetry and fiction)
ISBN 0-8018-7414-9 (pbk. : alk. paper)
1. Love stories, American. I. Title. II. Series.
PS3604.A954 C35 2003
813′.6 — dc21   2002154021

The following stories have been previously published: "A Night
Dive," *Baltimore Review*, Winter 2001; "Snapdragon," *Boulevard*,
Spring 1999; "Talent Show," *Mississippi Review Online*, June 1997.

A catalog record for this book is available from the British Library.

To Mary

Contents

Cake

Andromeda

The way newlyweds die: The honeymoon in Ixtapa, rising early from a sleepless night of lovemaking they wander hand in hand to the hotel pool, intending to guiltily dip away the night's sweat upon sweat before their breakfast of mango wedges, sips of dark coffee, an experimental chimichanga. They come upon the renal pool, one distant lowered lip allowing its water to slip to a pool lower, then to one below that, then to the Pacific and away. It is dawn secluded, just as they imagined it would be. Except, no! The white-clad figure of a pool attendant floats face down in the blue water. His brown ankles peek from between his white trousers and white canvas shoes. In his outstretched hand he still grasps the skimmer. The young husband is fit, crew-cropped, handsome, and tanned from tennis and weekend golf. He is also dangerously drunk from his recent extended sexual triumph, a campaign of huge field and intense combat, a tiny Noh play on an oversized bed against the only purely willing combatant he has ever known. Distended, sore, sleepless, but alive with the power that only carnal vigor can afford, he does not pause. A natural athlete, in three long steps, he sheds his barely buttoned shirt and flopping shoes and launches to save the life of the peasant. But for birth and education, sufficient protein, and a missed diagnosis early in childhood, this worker could be he—the guest, the gringo, the newlywed: fit, clever, a beautiful wife, and a full life spread like a royal flush on the blue baize below his lifesaving dive.

There is a black-spiked prick of unseen evil coiled in an Andromedan grotto of the gardenia-flecked pool. Like a serpent's tail it twists beneath the surface. Her breath drawn deeply, the young wife watches. Her husband's perfectly sculpted abdomen, where not an hour before she had rested her tired head, flexes in his powerful but futile arc toward the cruelly still water. Crude, unstepped Mexican electricity pulses through it, making its blue bed vitally alive.

As in the way I died when I met you, seated at a small round table in the sun, wearing white, a gold chain, and a ring set with a nacreous opal, the current coursed through me as I met your eye, a polluted, pregnant pool. But rather than suffer sudden convulsive death, I became a sybaritic Sisyphus, hanging forever upon the lip of your bougainvillea-ringed and electricity-ruined pool. Each day I push my tear-stained rock to Silex's craggy summit, a task I perform by simply focusing the jangly currents of my own lost and wasted brain.

Talent Show

Hates herself, runs away up to Washington, D.C., becomes a naked dancer at a talent show four blocks from the White House. Hates herself, runs away from home to Los Angeles, California, appears in two or so pornos, knocks around, lives for four years with an automobile mechanic in Santa Monica. Settles finally in Fresno, working for the state. Later she volunteers on a rape hotline.

Hates herself, stays home in Westmoreland County, Virginia. Drops out of high school and marries a boy whose family runs the county's school busses. No children. Lives out the rest of her life in her maternal grandmother's house, left to her when her grandmother dies.

Hates herself, stays home, finishes high school. Attends UVa, plays varsity soccer two years, quits after indeterminate benching, but keeps small scholarship money. Meets a boy from Baltimore, a lacrosse player. After graduation, she follows him back to that city, where he plans on being a writer. Under pressure from his parents, he attends law school six years later as a "mature student." She leaves him during finals in the spring of his second year. They were together for twelve years.

Hates herself, graduates valedictorian from high school in

Westmoreland County, Virginia, is admitted on early decision to Yale. It is the first instance of this from her high school, according to her college counselor. Goes to Yale and studies biology. Twice suffers nonconsensual intercourse, the second time at the hands of four premed majors with whom she studies organic chemistry. Dates a lacrosse payer her senior year, tells him one night of the acquaintance rapes. He is shot to death late the next evening, while walking home from a party.

Graduates fourth in her class from Westmoreland High, is admitted to Yale. Receives a "reputation" there her freshman year which, though embarrassing, she admits to herself is deserved. Twice finds herself in sexual situations so distasteful that, subsequent to each, she experiences severe depressions marked by incidences of self-mutilation. These she attributes—both times—to different roommates' cats. Is recognized by the faculty as an intense student. After graduation, works two years in Baltimore as manager of an adult literacy center. Returns to attend Yale Law. While studying there becomes engaged to a medical resident in New Haven. One night, she discovers her fiancé and three other men—residents as well—having sex with two exotic dancers at a large bachelor party held in her home to celebrate the engagement of one of their colleagues.

Westmoreland County High, fourth in class, Yale, Baltimore Literacy Project, returns to Yale law, engagement to a surgery resident. Breaks engagement for reasons never made clear to family or friends. Graduates law school and is appointed to a much-sought-after clerkship, working for a future Supreme Court justice on the D.C. bench. Two years later takes a job with the International Monetary Fund, then, two years after that, moves to the Washington offices of a major international investment bank. One night she joins two colleagues and two prominent clients at a business dinner. Afterward, on something of a dare, she joins them in visiting a naked dancing club that is four blocks from the White House.

Sits at the runway between the clients. Watches with a nervous smile as a stalky young woman wearing nothing but high heels and a gold chain around her waist grasps a smeared brass pole. The dancer wraps a bare leg over the shoulder of one of the clients.

A Night Dive

Is he an alcoholic? Thirty-four years old and a successful attorney employed by a respected midtown firm. "Alcoholics" have late-onset diabetes, middle-aged noses like anthills, and shocked white hair. They are hopeless types—or teenagers bullied into recovery by pestering relatives. But when he makes six figures? Is he an alcoholic? He's being divorced by his wife. She left him at Thanksgiving. Effectively single, he has been dating a senior in college. Her parents suspect—and are furious—especially the mother. How did it all happen? How did he get here from there? She's a Literature and Society major at Brown. Came to New York for summer to answer phones at a numbing, false-promise "internship." Wanted to be near her boyfriend, a conquer-the-world type working as a summer associate at the firm. Stanford Law, rising second year. When he first sees her, she is with her boyfriend at one of the firm's functions. He talks to her that first time. He is good that way. Second time comes after work. Everyone meets for drinks downstairs. He buys her a drink. They sit together in a little eddy of seats off from the main tumble: would-be lawyers imitating perfectly, with perfect coaching, what they will become. On the third meeting—a charm, again downstairs—he sneaks her off in a cab. They leave upon such a sudden impulse that she forgets her sweater on the chair. He goes back the next day to get it. Her thing with the summer associate is over. He changed his mind about her after beginning his internship. She just wanted an "ending." That was: not July. The first of August: Colorado Day. How did he get here from there? People ask. Of course, no one says "alcoholic." "Drinking problem" is used sometimes. "Drinks too much" is the usual. "Drinks too much," he thinks, used to be called "hard drinker." She's a senior at Brown University. Smart girl. Not sweet—has an acid tongue. Her parents suspect the relationship. He calls her in Bala Cynwyd. After the breakup Seanna—her name—has returned to her parents' house to get ready for school. Her mother answers. She sounds suspicious. Probably has been suspicious since her daughter turned twelve. He and Seanna talk for a long time. Is there a pickup while they speak? He can't remember. Certainly not at a compromising moment. Mother must have asked, who called? Daughter twenty-one, after all. Financially dependent still on parents, of course. Tall, good looks, athletic, speaks French and Italian. Likes to cook. What's her angle? With him? First there's the revenge factor. Might get back to boyfriend (ex), the world-conquering hero of Stanford Law, two years older, by picking up with a partner. Mother in real estate. Father—not real father—is a middling exec at Sun Oil in Philadelphia. Mother got pregnant at twenty. By a local boy during family's summer vacation on the Jersey Shore. Real father must have been some hunk of beach: the kid's a doll and built out of bricks. Mother didn't marry until Seanna was ten: It took that long. She calls him: midnight, one A.M. She is in Bala Cynwyd. Lonely, bored. Fighting with her mother. *What happened?* asks her mother. Conquer-the-world boyfriend, grew up in Rye or Greenwich or whatever. *That's* what her mother pays full-tuition to Brown for. He dropped her. Why? What did he see? During Stanford spring break he flew her into Palo Alto from Florence—over the Pole. Her junior year abroad. Working from Italy she found herself a lame and transparent internship so that she might be near him for the summer. By similar means sublet a studio on Twelfth Street. A convertible at

front, galley kitchen and smelly yellow bath behind. First time is
on the floor of the sublet. After the sweater on the chair. He helps
her make the hideaway but doesn't stay. He is *okay* that night: thrill
of the chase, chastised by papers served on him just that afternoon.
She was a large nondescript black woman waiting in the seventeenth
floor lobby. "Are you—?" she asks. "Yes," he says before he knows
what he's done. She serves him his divorce. Quite decent, really, the
way she handles it. He's got two summer associates standing there
and two receptionists watching. Maybe the receptionists understand what is happening. Not the summer associates. Bomb could
go off, his brains could squirt out his ears; the summer associates
wouldn't understand. What's in it for her? For Seanna Sternwood?
Isn't he an alcoholic? Being divorced, papers served by his wife.
How did he get there? From Del Norte, Colorado, to white-shoe
firm, midtown, six figures, drinks too much? Played rugby at Stanford. It was his great aunt who sent him. Rugby players drank too
much. He drank like a rugby player. At his fighting weight, he
looked as if he could gain a hundred pounds and still look fit. He
didn't gain a hundred pounds. He gained eighty. Played rugby and
drank. Now, mostly, he drinks. Lifts weights Tuesday, Thursday
mornings. Hung-over, eyes swollen, stomach up in his chest. The
pulse in his forehead rings like the splash of water against the hull
of an aluminum skiff. Clank of weights on weights. Dry thump of
dumbbells against the rubber-padded floor. The ripped benches.
The mirrors. The smells. Plays racquetball on Fridays. He hates
racquetball. He calls Bala Cynwyd. Her mother answers: a hawk,
fluttering nervously always around the phone. She recognizes his
voice. Twice he has called before. *What is he thinking? He is thirty-
four.* Seanna picks up in another room. The first extension never
cuts out. As he speaks, he can tell. It's obvious, really. He remembers it from talking to his grandparents as a child. Both on the line
at once. No mistaking it. Can't hear her well. He watches what he
says: no double meanings or intimate references or word play. Not
too formal, either. No blowing like a con on the phone in the vis-

iting room at jail. Just a brief organization of their next "lunch" on the Friday of her upcoming weekend "friends." She plays along. Does she know her mother might be listening? He says good-bye formally, then waits for the line to close—a click, then, just after, the wan beep of a portable handset powered down. Mother listening all along. What is happening? What happened? Conquer-the-world boyfriend ended their relationship at the end of July. He's tall, slim, redheaded, and grew up Norwalk—skis, plays squash. Wealthy family. Summer associate. In the real estate section, working with other lawyers. Meets him just once. A kid. Could have snatched her from him, under other circumstances. Only, *he* dropped her. Why? The drinking makes him think such thoughts. What's wrong? He drinks too much. Became obvious five years before. Given a backwater case to try that grew, by unforeseen events, to be huge. Two years he works at it. It eats through him. First his gut. Then his legs. Finally, his head. Like some voracious bacteria, it feeds on his flesh. He is replaced. First by a partner, then by a senior partner. It nearly sinks *him*—the senior partner—too. Case changes firms. Nobody's ticket, after all. From that time on he swings gingerly, the severely beaned batsman who never gets it back. How did it happen? He's no dummy. Stanford. Georgetown Law. Athletic. Drinks too much. Going through a divorce. Wife serves the papers on the first day of August. Colorado Day. Her decision is final. It's over. Later that month, on the weekend before Labor Day, Seanna visits him. Hot. No hint of autumn yet in the air. He leaves work at noon. Cancels racquetball. Meets her at Penn Station. She wants to come to midtown, to appear at the firm and leave with him. He meets her instead. She's lovely—dressed all in black linen, sleeveless blouse, and trousers. Carries a black Gladstone and a bucket bag in black leather. Lit and Society. Reads French, doesn't talk much about it. Telephone rings at his place that evening around nine. They're in bed, under the air conditioning, thinking of getting up, getting out for some dinner. It's her roommate from Providence on the phone, a New York girl, home for the summer. She's the friend Seanna's meant to be visiting. They speak briefly. Your mother knows, says the roommate. She's looking for you. Seanna hangs up. The next call comes right away. She hasn't moved. Slim, naked, long-legged, she sits at the middle of the bed. Her legs tucked under her. Answers it herself. Her mother. How does she know? His number? Call waiting—or, of course: from the long distance bills. He listens, watching while she talks. Watches her in the pinkness of her unselfconscious and firm nudity until he hears his own name. He showers. His arms hurt from lifting the day before. There is a bite mark on his flabby waist. "Drinks too much." When he drinks, he becomes belligerent. He knows this. Goes with her to the train station. Back to Bala Cynwyd. There will be no "weekend" after all. Mother intends for Seanna to go to medical school even though her major is Lit and Society. Along with Proust and Gide, D'Annunzio, and Moravia she has taken chemistry, organic chemistry, biochemistry, molecular cell biology, calculus, physics, and done lab work in dermatology. On her medical boards she scored 34—quite high—and received the best writing score possible. Wants to go to Stanford Med. For ten years she and her mother lived in cheap condos in New Jersey. Her mother worked as an executive secretary and dated. She kept Seanna in group daycare until she was seven, when she became latchkey. For all of this, Seanna feels she owes her mother everything. Outside Penn Station it is a wonderful night in New York, obscenely hot, heavy, and fluid. He feels as if he is on a skin dive through the most marvelous reef. A night dive. What creatures live there! While making love, he bit the nape of her neck. It was in response to the bite on his side. Would leave a mark, he knew. Like a moray eel in its hole. One bites you, you swim to the surface, hack its head off with a dive knife—the only way to end the clench. He hadn't held on. Quick to strike, he had released as easily. Home. Falls asleep. When he goes to work on Monday, the summer associates have all gone. Spends the week drinking and calling his wife and crying on the telephone, trying to persuade her to halt the divorce, to come back again. She tells him he "drinks too much." She tells him, I hate you, get some help. Early in the morning on the last Saturday of September, he rides the train to Providence. Takes a cab up College Hill to a small yellow clapboard house. An elm, like a gigantic wheat sheaf, stands in front. Her roommate opens the door—a pretty, sophisticated blond woman who wants to be an actress. He knows her father, but he doesn't bother her with that. Seanna comes out. They drive in her car along the Narragansett Bay. The sky looks painted and the tilting autumn light colors everything a valedictory gold. They stop in a pretty town with brightly colored houses and an ancient graveyard, where thick green turf grows between the crumbling stones. Indians fish off the pier, speaking an unfamiliar language. She leans over the painted railing and looks into the inky water. The Indians fish with only string and bait. He notices a fading purple bruise peek from above the collar of her white linen shirt. Still barely there. They eat dinner at Narragansett Pier. He proposes all sorts of wild scenarios. He proposes. She leaves him at the train station in Westerly.

Crazy Yvonne

Sophie cut the legs off the coffee table. She did it with a hacksaw that Richard kept in the broom closet. The coffee table, a Chippendale reproduction bought secondhand on Greenmount Avenue, was on coasters. Sophie wanted the coasters off. They offended her. One day, she sawed them. When she'd finished making the legs even—she could be meticulous and fussy about things—the table stood a mere six inches off the floor.

Richard arrived home to find a half-empty bottle of wine sitting open on the kitchen counter. Sophie was in the bedroom. The door was closed. Next he noticed the coffee table, shamefully hugging the floor.

After they had a big fight, Richard sat alone in the bedroom, on the edge of the bed, staring out the window onto a chilly and bare St. Paul Street. Sophie was in the living room, watching a DVD on Richard's laptop, listening to the soundtrack over headphones.

Before going to bed, he came out of the bedroom for a glass of water. The living room was dark, except for the glow of the laptop's flickering screen. He didn't even look in Sophie's direction. Then, in the dark, he collided with her, who at that moment was emerging from the galley kitchen.

"Shit!" she yelled. "You *idiot!*" When Richard flipped on the kitchen light, he saw that she had been carrying a plastic tumbler, the kind designed to be used near pools. It had been full of wine, and a lot of it had sloshed onto her blouse and over the floor. "You clean it up," she said.

With nothing more than a backhand flick, not even a jab, Richard struck the glass from Sophie's hand. Unfortunately, she'd been lifting the cup to drink and it caught her square in the mouth. With a slow-motion incredulity, the plastic cup now at her feet in an even worse skid of wine, she touched the pad of her left ring finger to her lip. She pulled it away to display velvety red blood. Richard could see the vertical cut across her lip, and more blood blooming from it.

He took a towel, wrapped three ice cubes into a compress, and held it against her cut, praying against stitches. The next morning, she went to stay with a girlfriend, her only one in Baltimore. Her name was Katie, a thin, translucent-skinned heiress from California who took Sophie on orgiastic shopping sprees when her medications were out of whack. She had an impressively big apartment in an old and rat-infested building in midtown.

They hardly communicated for the next two weeks. At first Richard was remorseful that he'd hit her, then grateful to be alone. A little later he began to feel lonely, spending night after night at the sticky bar of the Blue Jay Grill, trying to find interest in the professional hockey or basketball that bubbled colorfully through the smoky murk above the bar. It felt as if not just Sophie, but the entire world had left him behind. They had been together two years. Suddenly it seemed to him that being with her would be slightly less painful than being apart.

Twice he tried calling her at Katie's place, and both times there was no answer. He didn't leave messages. Lying in bed at night, he concocted all sorts of self-lacerating scenarios: Katie had taken Sophie to a winetasting—Katie was always going to winetastings—where Sophie had met someone. He'd be a lawyer, Richard suspected, whom she slept with after a proper date the next night and in whose apartment she was now probably living in Federal Hill. Or Katie had taken Sophie to a winetasting where Sophie met someone from the art institute, brought him back to Katie's big apartment, and was now living with him in his loft in Sowebo. Or Katie had taken Sophie to a winetasting—and on and on like that, sometimes for hours on end.

One evening he saw some people he knew at the Blue Jay Grill. The Blue Jay was the sort of place where you might know a lot of people there and yet be friendly with none of them. This group was different. Richard had actually hung out with some of them before—a rollicky guy named Tom, who lived as a boarder in a fraternity house, and a tall, redheaded girl with him, whose name was Camille but was also called, for some reason, Sparkle. The rest of the group—three girls—he didn't recognize. Tom could be a bit much—he was a mooch and his life at the frat was embarrassingly juvenile—but Richard was so grateful for the chance to spend the evening with somebody, anybody, that he gladly joined in.

They marched around town—the six of them crushed inside Tom's ailing silver Saab, Sparkle always on Richard's lap—and at each bar or faltering party they lost a member of the group. Finally it was just Tom and Sparkle, and they ended up on the floor of Richard's apartment, drinking wine around the stunted coffee table. From the floor, the table's height made a certain amount of sense, like something in a Japanese restaurant. Richard was drifting in and out of the conversation, which was largely Tom trying to seduce Sparkle.

"I started at Hobart," he said. "On a lacrosse scholarship."

"Really?" Sparkle asked, playing with a strand of her red hair. "They're good, aren't they?" Sparkle wasn't from Baltimore, but living in Baltimore, at least this part of Baltimore, brought with it a certain amount of reverence for lacrosse.

"Good, but not that year." Richard knew that Tom had never been to Hobart. He also knew that he had never played lacrosse. "So I transferred down here. I played my second year, but then I blew out my knee."

"Really?" Sparkle asked him, inching, it seemed to Richard, closer to the presumably injured knee. Tom didn't remotely resemble a varsity collegiate athlete. He resembled a guy in his mid-twenties who still lived in a college fraternity house.

"I quit after that," he said. "It wasn't worth it to me to risk really ruining my knee forever. As it is, I'll probably walk like an old man by the time I'm forty."

Richard thought that Sparkle was going to kiss Tom's forehead there and then.

"Didn't you guys win that year?" Richard asked, pouring out more wine. Tom looked at him for a long time. "Win" in Baltimore meant the national championship. Tom didn't even know what year he was talking about, in his fantasized collegiate career. Sparkle held on expectantly for an answer.

"It's all history now," Tom said. Richard felt bad for him. He didn't mean to ruin his chances with Sparkle. Tom got up from the floor, went to the bathroom, and when he came out, said that he was going to split. Sparkle hardly moved. Richard got up and saw him to the door. He just wanted to make certain there were no hard feelings.

When he got back on the floor with Sparkle, there didn't seem much else to do but kiss her. She kissed him back enthusiastically: She was a good kisser. Was it that she liked him more than Tom or that it just didn't matter? He hadn't been with anyone but Sophie for so long that it was fun at first—the different taste, the feel of a different mouth, the sudden surprise of the asymmetry of her breasts. They were both drunk, the ceiling lights blared above, and the shades in the windows were not drawn. They plowed ahead without much art. In no time her shirt was off, and he was struggling with her ugly bra. She went so far as to unbuckle his pants and then unbutton them, but no farther. He unzipped her snug jeans, and she cooperated by lifting her hips from the carpet to facilitate their removal. She wore a thong in a desert camouflage pattern.

With her pants off she said, "Tomorrow is my birthday."

Richard lay beside her, searching for an answer through the cotton-bud haze.

"Maybe we could hang out," she said. "Do this then."

He walked her home; it was only across the boulevard and up two blocks to a sixties apartment tower that made his own block look dowdier still.

Richard met Yvonne Kelly the next evening, Sparkle's birthday. He had Sparkle's number in the pocket of his jeans, but he didn't call it. By eight, when he figured that she'd made other plans (if she'd ever actually contemplated spending her birthday with him), he jogged across the street to the Blue Jay Grill. It was raining hard and Richard carried one of Sophie's collapsible umbrellas. Yvonne was standing inside the Blue Jay's door. She surprised Richard as he paused to shake out his umbrella; it was almost as if she had materialized there to startle him. They began talking immediately. All the awkward preliminaries were washed away. She was smart *and* funny. After chatting amiably for a while, Richard lent her Sophie's umbrella. She had been waiting by the door for the rain to ease.

Richard did call Yvonne, the next afternoon. The umbrella's return became the ostensible reason for their second meeting. They chose the Blue Jay again because it was mutually familiar.

Yvonne arrived promptly, just a few moments after he'd walked through the door. She carried the folded umbrella. They got a table and he paid for two beers. After an hour or so of drinking and talking, Richard suggested they go somewhere for dinner. Dinner had never been a factor in the initial equation, but he made the offer with confidence. It was going well. Yvonne accepted the offer so readily, it might have been her idea.

"Where would you like?" he asked.

"Sushi?" she suggested.

"Sure," he said. It wasn't his idea of much, but he was certain not to run into Sophie there, which concerned him a little. Sophie thought that sushi was a health hazard.

They found a cab almost immediately, on St. Paul Street, just outside the Blue Jay's door. It was a short ride—to midtown only. When he crawled out to the curb, he felt a swell of happiness for the first time in a long while. She was pretty in a way he'd always been attracted to: dark, wavy hair and deep-blue eyes. She smiled contentedly; she was happy to be on a date with him. They were on a *date*, going to a restaurant to eat together.

They followed the hostess, who wobbled happily side to side on her wooden clogs. At their table, almost immediately, the sushi began. Richard ordered more beer, a Japanese brand that came in pint cans. He didn't have much of an appetite. But he ate. He wanted to please Yvonne. The sushi kept coming. Yvonne ordered and she ordered confidently and copiously. He ate what she ordered. The waitress sailed happily between their table and the bar. Richard lost track. The room began to flutter. More and more sushi arrived, always on boat-shaped plates, and more beer. He tried to steady his vision upon the walls, but the rice screens only caused his head to swim more. Each time he looked down, four additional pieces of fish appeared, tied with seaweed to small beds of rice. Here she came again, the waitress, looking like a Japanese flag, porcelain white with a giant red target at her middle. Yvonne took the two little ships from her hands.

Now they were on to sake, poured from what looked like a salt shaker into matching thimbles.

Finally, Yvonne said, "Just one more."

The waitress arrived with the finale. It was a tiny black eel, asleep on a little white pillow of rice. Richard ate it, then immediately wished that he hadn't.

The bill came. Richard put in onto an unsteady credit card. After an anxious wait, the waitress wobbled back with the slip, which he signed, and they left the restaurant.

Outside, they decided to walk for a while, along Charles Street. The air felt alive. Traffic glided. Richard's head pounded. Though February, and now past eleven, it was mild. They drifted into each other's arms. They were on a *date:* drinks, the expensive, impressive dinner, the wandering home together. A new world opened before him: of dates, and get-togethers, and the meeting of new people.

They came to the brightly lit train station. The blocks ahead could be dangerous, so they entered the back of the first cab waiting in a thin rank of Ukrainian and Sikh drivers. He took them up Charles Street to her building, the same in which Sparkle lived.

"You're coming up, right?" she asked after he'd paid the driver. The lights beneath the building's canopy were comically bright. Yvonne wore a long wool coat. Her purse was strapped crosswise over her shoulders. Richard could see his own building skulking down the street, lights burning in only a few windows. Many of the tenants were elderly.

"Do you have something to drink?" he asked. It came out nearly involuntarily, as if some other person were speaking. They rode up in the building's elevator. Now he had two women he'd prefer not to see: It seemed inevitable to him that the door would open onto a disapproving Sparkle, or perhaps Sparkle and Sophie standing together.

It didn't, however. Her apartment was a nice one. She had a fawn-colored carpet and a stylish sofa. True to the building's flying-saucer curves, the door to the balcony had vertical blinds. Framed photographs hung on the walls—black-and-white pictures whose subjects were impossible to resolve in the dim light. She dropped her purse and coat on a chair inside the door and then pulled a bottle of wine from a small rack on the counter. Richard opened the wine with the corkscrew she handed him. She produced two glasses. He poured them each some.

Plainly, they were going to bed. All that remained was the end game of it. Richard sat on the sofa. The blinds were not drawn, and the downtown's riverine lights twinkled. Yvonne remained standing. Richard wanted this part to last—the romantic moment of surrender, when self-interest converged upon an honest desire to please and to be pleasurable. He wanted to see the moment of recognition as it flashed across a grateful face. Yvonne walked without a word into the bedroom. She began undressing. Richard hurried after her. Quickly, they were naked. She pulled him to the bed, and they fell to the sheets. A hatched blue glow ran across the floor. They were both naked, in a bed together with the rest of the night before them, and yet they had not even kissed. Richard kissed her, kisses that she returned in only a perfunctory way. This was the other side of dating, he supposed—the awkward uncovering, the discovery of strange marks, odd habits, and disconcerting opinions. The part where what had seemed such a wonderful match over cocktails turned in to a crummy quarrel at dessert.

She had broad shoulders but sharp elbows, hips, and knees. Her skin felt clammy. In his exploratory embrace she went rigid. Because he was drunk, he wondered if he had misunderstood somehow her intentions. Yet, there they were, naked, in the dark, in her bed.

"Maybe I should go," he said after a moment of lying motionless side by side.

"No!" She pulled him forcefully on top her. With an almost gynecological efficiency, she began their lovemaking. It served him right, he assumed—for getting so drunk, for being here. He finished quickly then passed out beside her.

Richard had nothing in his mind when he woke at dawn. The truth of the situation, matted with nausea and hangover, came to him quickly enough. Yvonne stirred. The sheet covered her only to the waist. A quarter-sized mouse-brown bruise stood out violently on the inner side of her pale left breast.

"I know," she said, pulling the sheet to her chin and stifling a yawn. "It's embarrassing."

They showered together. She left him alone in the bathroom to towel dry. He opened the fogged-over cabinet above the sink, hoping to find an aspirin. On a glass shelf there sat a spool of thread with a needle stuck in, tweezers, and a small tube of wrinkle cream. Next to the crimped tube sat a prescription vial of lithium. Richard had never seen lithium before, but, like the electric chair, he recognized it immediately. To begin, it said "lithium" on the drug line. Next came her name, a recent date, and the twice-daily dosing instructions. He closed the cabinet door, only to see his own image, breaking through the fading condensation. He didn't want to be alone.

They went together downtown, to the harbor.

A shift of blue hung in the otherwise pillowy southern sky. The plaza was quiet, still, and reluctant. He and Yvonne held hands. At the window of a pizza restaurant in one of the Harbor Place pavilions, she suggested that they eat lunch. The sun drooped behind a lazy scrim above Federal Hill. It was early—they were the first customers. They both ordered calzones, which came on red-rimmed oval plates. Richard drank a glass of Orvieto. Out the window, the flat green of the harbor basin was flecked with darting gulls. Yvonne quickly ate her lunch, then finished his in ravenous gulps. Watching her, he felt himself slipping back into being drunk again. He ordered another glass of wine and paid for their lunch.

Outside, the light was an old-glass gray. The air had gotten colder. Yvonne tugged on the placket of Richard's wool overcoat, playfully pulling herself into him. She gave him a light hip-check, the first spontaneous bit of affection he'd experienced from her. Richard raised his head and smiled.

Sophie and her friend Katie stood ten yards ahead. Katie looked stunned. Sophie, however, had already gone past that. Richard could practically hear her teeth grinding. Her skin, always slow to heal, still looked off-color around her lower lip. He continued walking in her direction; there was little alternative. Yvonne dropped the hem of his overcoat.

"May I have a word with you?" Sophie asked when Richard reached her. What was he supposed to do?

Yvonne and Richard sat together on Yvonne's sofa, watching the last of the champagne light drain from over the city. The gathering Saturday dusk came so freighted with conflicting meaning. Richard slumped in her arms, pondering the smell of her moisturizer and the appliances—a blender, an espresso machine, and a toaster—that sat on the counter of her open kitchen. He was in the midst of explaining that he had a party to go to that evening.

In the weeks since the fight, he and Sophie had spoken only once—when she called to remind him that this Saturday her brother, her only sibling, would be visiting. Early into their relationship, Richard had signed on to a sort of confidentiality agreement: Sophie had very strict notions about dealing with her family. First, and perhaps obviously, they were not to know that Sophie and Richard lived together. Richard never answered the phone, which became quite natural after a while. Twice her parents had visited Baltimore, staying at a nice hotel on University Parkway. On each visit, Richard had accompanied them to a Friday night dinner and then Sunday brunch. He was Sophie's boyfriend and treated as such. Her parents struck him as a bit stiff, but no worse really than most other examples of the form. Sophie spoke of them only rarely. When she did, her accounts were mostly neutral.

Her brother as well had been kept mostly in the dark about their relationship. Now that it was over, she still chose to deceive him. Sophie insisted that they pretend to be together, until she decided exactly what to tell her parents. Still afraid of her making an issue of his hitting her—though by now Richard had convinced himself that it had been an accident—he agreed to spend this evening with Sophie and her brother, acting like a couple.

Richard didn't paint it to Yvonne in exactly these terms.

At first, she insisted that she be brought along. "I'm not going to let you treat me like this," she said, raising herself up into a sitting position. "I've let myself be treated this way before, but I'm not going to any more. I won't be just a convenience."

He wondered for a moment about telling her the truth—that would have gotten him easily free. But it felt like too big a tool for the job. Despite the bruise, the lithium, the curious sex, and the insatiable appetite, he wanted to see her again. He liked Yvonne Kelly.

Finally, she succumbed on her own. "I guess you were cool

about finding my bruise," she said. "We *are* just starting out."
Richard got up from the chair and walked to the window. Below, a
block down, the Blue Jay Grill awning stretched out from the building. Its scalloped aprons danced in the wind.

"I saw it, you know," Yvonne said, standing beside him. "One
morning last December. Remember? I was standing right here,
looking at that building for some reason when she appeared.
There," she pointed. "In a window on the top floor. She put her feet
out the window first, then sat for only a second on the sill. The way
she fell, at first I thought it was a mistake. Her legs kicked, like she
thought she that could swim back. It happened very quickly. She
landed on the canopy."

They kissed, embraced, and then Richard rode down the elevator and walked home.

Sophie was in the apartment, as if she'd never left. She had
come a couple of times before to collect things, but always when
Richard was out. There hadn't been evidence of her recently. She
sat with her brother in the living room, around the cowering coffee table. Richard said hello to Joseph, Sophie's brother, then excused himself to the bedroom. In the bathroom he took more aspirin and showered. Afterward, as he dressed, Sophie appeared. She
shut the door behind her and sat on the bed.

She petted the coverlet. "You slept with that woman. You had
sex with her, didn't you?"

"No," Richard said. "As a matter of fact, I didn't."

"She was holding your jacket!" Sophie spat back at him, grab-
bing a fistful of blanket. "Don't you *lie* to me."

They went to the party she had promised her brother. It was a
wearisome affair in a row house with three floors, a sky-lit stair, and
nine bedrooms. The inhabitants moved back and forth between
them, attaching and reattaching themselves, usually in an ill-
considered way. They all worked in pointless part-time jobs, like
being a bike mechanic or shelving books at the university library.
Richard, Sophie, and her brother sat the living room, where a

woman trashed her recent boyfriend. Sophie's brother listened intently, and Sophie herself looked pointedly at Richard with each fresh revelation of infidelity.

Richard rose to refill his drink. Sophie followed him.

"Why don't you just tell me," she said to him, pulling him by his shirt to a stop in the narrow passageway to the kitchen. She was a short woman, something he thought of only when they were standing at close quarters. "I won't mind, really. We were split up, if that's what's bothering you. I know that."

Richard poured the last of a bottle of vodka into his glass. It was the first time all day that he'd felt right. He squeezed a used lime wedge into the drink, added ice from a bag, and fished among the open bottles for tonic.

"There are things that I could tell you," Sophie said. "I haven't been a saint."

Sophie's brother spent the night on the sofa beside the wounded coffee table. Sophie slept with Richard.

In the morning her brother woke and dressed. Sophie called a cab for him. He was headed back to Kissimmee.

It was St. Valentine's Day.

"What are we doing for Valentine's?" Sophie asked when she returned from seeing her brother off in the lobby. Richard took her to brunch at the French restaurant in the apartment block on 39th Street. It was the place they generally went on special occasions. The dining room was crowded with extended families—young parents, their children, the children's grandparents—brunching. Richard and Sophie each drank two of the complimentary mimosas apiece and Sophie talked at length about her adventure with Katie Courant and their shopping expeditions and the never-ending problem with the rats in her gracious old building.

When they'd finished, Richard gave the waiter his credit card. A few moments later, the hostess, an elderly, heavy French woman who owned the place with her husband, returned with the card on a funereal black tray. It had been rejected, she was sorry to announce. Coloring, Richard gave her another.

Richard and Sophie walked back to their apartment across 39th Street. It was colder than the day before, more realistic for the season. The sky was a milky white. They didn't talk. At home, Richard read the Sunday paper that he'd bought at the deli across from the French restaurant. By late afternoon, Sophie had still not left for Katie's. Darkness fell. Richard went around closing the window shades.

"I'm going to work out," he said to her a little before eight.

Sophie was watching the television. She gave him a shrug when he said good-bye. Downstairs, in front of the building, Richard looked up to the apartment's window, half expecting to see the shade lifted and the top of Sophie's blonde head.

He was going to find Yvonne. On the short walk to her building, he considered the possibilities. It was Valentine's Day. She might be out; she might have someone in her apartment with her—there was the bruise, which had never been spoken further of. More likely, Richard sensed, she'd be there alone, dressed in flannel pajama bottoms and an old boyfriend's oxford-cloth, her hair up, eyeglasses on. She would be waiting, hoping that Richard would come to her, the way a new boyfriend would. It was St. Valentine's Day. The weather felt colder still. A low, overcast sky glowed above the streetlights. Some sort of front had blown in. It smelled like snow. He hadn't worn enough jacket.

At Yvonne's building, he stood for a time at the door before ringing. Everything twinkled beneath the surreally bright lights of the canopy. A low white car with tinted windows, fat alloy rims, and thumping music pulled to a stop behind him. No one got out; the car simply idled, quivering like a cat in the cold. A tall, slim woman wearing a leather jacket appeared at the door. It was Sparkle.

"Hey," she said to him as she opened the second set of doors. She took a cigarette out of her purse and lit it.

"Hey," he said.

"What are *you* doing here?"

"I was going up to see . . . " He hesitated. "I was going to visit someone."

"Oh, please, tell me that it isn't Crazy Yvonne."

Richard looked past her into the shining lobby, all yellowish marble and brass.

"It *is?*" she asked.

"I guess," he said. "Yes, Yvonne."

"Oh, Richard," she said. "Don't you know that she just got out of the hospital again?" She smoked her cigarette and waved her hand. "Eating disorder, et cetera."

Sparkle pressed her lips together, as if to even out her plum-colored lipstick. The window of the shivering white car retracted evenly. A kid with short hair, a gold chain, and a slim moustache leaned on an elbow across the passenger seat.

"*What?*" she said to him. The driver slumped back into his bucket seat, but the window remained down. "Well?" she said to Richard. "Go. She's probably up there waiting. Standing on her balcony." Sparkle twisted her head to an unattractive angle and brought her face close to his. "*Waiting*," she said, making her eyes scarily large.

Her heels clicked on the pavement. The kid in the T-shirt revved the engine. A taxicab pulled up behind him beneath the canopy. A small old woman climbed from the back of the cab. She was wearing a turquoise wool overcoat nearly as long as she was tall. Sparkle opened the door of the low, glossy car and climbed in. With a screech, the white car popped out into the dark street. The woman in the turquoise overcoat looked after the car, then at Richard. Using a single key from her small pocketbook she let herself into the building.

The first tentative flakes of a winter's storm began to fall. The last piece of sushi he ate with Yvonne came to mind—a sleeping eel tied by seaweed to a tiny pillow of white rice. The thought made his tongue swell, and his mouth watered in a disconcerting way. He felt as if he might be sick. The tires of the cars on the street began leaving tracks in the quickly falling snow.

Buena Vista Notebook

In French, *sale* = vile.

In Yiddish, *dinner* = thinner.

Like pearls before Tiburon.

Melancholy, cold and dry, thick, black, and sour.

The smell of condom on a spring morning.

Other men's wives, liberated by Chardonnay, who insist on kissing you in the front seats of their cars, parking in the Embarcadero garage or beneath Union Square.

She sleeps over, then stays the next morning through breakfast. Performs her daily ablutions and then returns to sitting on the sofa. The pages of the *Chronicle* turn, waiting for her to leave.

Japanese people, when finished with a telephone conversation, say, "I'm sorry I've disgusted you!"

In Israel, moments of elation are recorded by exclaiming *Swimming pool!*

French people, when they are angry with one another, point and say *Jacuzzi!*

Putting on a tuxedo: cummerbund with gills up, as if to hold theater tickets there. From *kamar-band*, Hindi-Persian for loincloth.

Venus's Girdle: a ribbon-shaped marine animal with a jellylike bluish-green iridescent body.

And this from 1688: "French kick-shows, cellery, and Champain."

Vogel, Ger., little bird; *faigela*, Yiddish slang, male homosexual, thus *fag*.

The three great annoyances of wolves, rattlesnakes, and mosquitos.

Orgasm is "high tide" in Mandarin Chinese.

Doxy = mistress.

Doxology = hymn of praise.

Matilda the Pun.

The later alphabet contains two Anglo-Saxon treasures: *wen* and *thorn*. Wen came to be known as the "double-u" from the French description of its appearance. However, the connection is spurious. Thorn is the digraph *th*, most commonly seen in *ye*. Consequently, *ye*, as in *ye old England*, should be pronounced "the old England."

Span-new, from the Icelandic, literally, chip-new, thus bran new, brand new.

Wine merchant at the Buena Vista Market says of a bottle of champagne: "It's rather fruity."

"I get enough *fruity* every day," the customer says.

A mild enzymatic solution.

Queer, from *Queer Street?* Cf. *OED:* "an imaginary street where people in difficulties reside; hence, any difficulty, fix or trouble, bad circumstances, debt, illness, etc." Partridge puts *queer* in usage for a male homosexual as an American variation, circa 1930s. The exclusive association of *Queer Street* with financial difficulties alone has never been the case. Rather, it is a small aspect of the phrase, derived undoubtedly from a noun sense of *queer* as counterfeit paper money (while *bogus* implies counterfeit specie). Thus *queer as a three-dollar bill*. The forward formation of *queer* to indicate homosexual can hardly be taken as either random or coming as late as the 1930s or exclusively American.

Henry is living in San Francisco with Justice. She works for a recording studio in Russian Hill. Justice is the sort of woman, in her mid-twenties, attractive and smart, who works at an under-performing job, just a receptionist, really, because she believes that somehow her talents—of which there are many but none consonant with the recording industry—will shine through eventually. Nearly every man who walks through the chocolate-brown lobby plays on her. The walls are decorated with gold records. Justice is having an affair; it began within weeks of her beginning the job.

Henry is living in San Francisco with Justice. Although also only in his mid-twenties, this is not the first time that one of his girl-friends has been sleeping with someone else. It's a condition of the age, he supposes, to be no longer teenaged and idealistic, but not yet saddled with early-thirties weight gain and responsibility. To be cal-low, clueless, and confused. He doesn't understand why she hasn't left him. Justice is sleeping with another man—men, possibly. She's gotten thin, thinner even than usual: It's her French Canadian showing through. The flintiness. The skinflintiness. They've stopped having sex; rather, they have it rarely and only at her suf-ferance. Her eyes dance in her head. They drive to Bolinas on their "anniversary." Henry opens a bottle of champagne on a foam-flecked beach. The wind blows sand in their eyes. Justice begins to cry.

Henry is living in San Francisco with Justice. One August evening, he walks from the Embarcadero, where he works, to the top of Russian Hill. Henry suspects the studio's owner, a divorcé in his later thirties with an eight-year-old daughter. He has an apartment in the building, and at first Justice spoke a great deal of the occasions, many in a day, on which she'd be sent up there. Files, tapes, computer disks, a wrapped gift from Gump's; once, disas-trously, dry cleaning. She let him know that she wasn't going to touch his dry cleaning. "But the views, Henry," she says, calling him at work while on one of the errands upstairs, *"Bridge to bridge!"* At a certain point, before he becomes suspicious, she stops talking of her trips to the apartment upstairs. It is as if they had stopped happening. But he knows that they haven't. Lost as he is in thought as he climbs the final hill, Henry bumps into a man. He is Elliot

Eckard, the rock star. They were introduced once, in passing, at the studio. He has been working all summer on his new project at Russian Hill Studios. They collide forcefully, and Henry's charcoal gray suit, conservative tie, and black shoes at a high shine—the appurtenances of the junior broker that he is—do not seem to convince Eckard that he hasn't been assaulted. His eyes popping, he looks at Henry with something very close to panic. Henry apologizes profusely, holding up a hand and his briefcase, which is more prop than actual conveyance, to signal his own startled fault. Finally Eckard nods and continues down the hill.

Justice leaves Henry in San Francisco. She goes to live with her mother in Devon, Pennsylvania. After she has been gone two months, Henry starts seeing an old girlfriend who is in graduate school at Stanford. It is a doomed relationship. Henry then dates a woman from Marin County. Next comes an old friend who lives in Cole Valley. None of them interests him: He's only trying to find some alternative to Justice. It's like getting the flu when he thinks about her—the rising fever, the sore eyes, the nausea. It hurts him physically, the thought of her. It hurts in his head and at the top of his stomach and in his joints. It makes his legs ache.

Justice leaves Henry in San Francisco. Henry meets a woman he knew in Providence. He recognizes her sitting in a coffee shop below Market. They trade numbers; she's just moved back to San Francisco and is living with her parents in the Marina. Henry has her over for dinner. Another week they meet at a club on Sutter. When she has her birthday, she invites Henry to a party at her mother's club, the Pacific League on Union Square. There are cocktails in the library, followed by dinner in the main dining room. Just after the entrée is served to the four tables of ten, Henry excuses himself and returns to the library, where he picks up a copy of the *Los Angeles Times*. He and the woman aren't even friends. He is lonely, and she feels sorry for him. He falls asleep and immediately begins dreaming of being without her, without Justice, and of being happy. He dreams of not noticing even that she is gone.

A woman approaches and taps him gently on the arm. The newspaper lies across his lap. He awakens at her touch.

"Henry," she says. "Remember me?"

Justice leaves Henry in San Francisco. He begins sleeping with a woman. She is separated from her husband, who is in Santa Fe, pursuing his interest in motorcycles, extreme skiing, and Indian jewelry. First they spend stillborn weekends together. Next she begins arriving each night, in the dark and the rain, after she has finished work. His landlords, who live in the house above his apartment, recognize her car. On a Sunday afternoon, she and Henry sit in a bar in the Embarcadero. She tells him that she has only loved three men in her life. None is her husband. One is a doctor with whom she had an affair. One is a man whom she never even kissed, and one is Henry. They sit on a wide elevated walkway connecting buildings. What is she proposing? She doesn't exactly know. They wander up Columbus Avenue through a creepy stillness and raking late-winter light. But for perfunctory intercourse, in all honesty there has been nothing in it for Henry. To him, together they are no more than a matrix of null figures. She wants Henry to stay in San Francisco and move into her flat, still hung with photographs taken by her shutterbug husband. Henry hates the place, with its pressed-tin ceilings, scuffed wooden floors, and magazines fanned on the coffee table in the sitting room. The bathroom has Swiss-dot curtains. The bedroom's sheets smell of medicated rubs.

At the tops of buildings, flags stand out in a sharp breeze. The sky is cloudless. They walk up the deserted avenue. A valedictory gold has begun to blossom in the buildings' upper windows. The bay, when visible, is a defiant blue. In the empty cross streets, newspapers swirl like movie extras. Sunlight ebbs. Lights begin to flicker on. The wind seeps further into the streets, heavy with the metallic scent of February. It begins to turn cold. The season is asserting itself, along with Sunday sadness and grim news. They walk on to her flat, just behind Van Ness, arm in arm. To the bystander, they might resemble people in love.

One year later, Henry and two acquaintances are viewing an exhibit at the Walters Art Museum in Baltimore. The show, Dutch paintings from Utrecht, is divided between two galleries, separated by an inner courtyard. Henry briefly loses his two companions, captivated by the last painting in the first gallery, *Andromeda*, by Wtewael. It disturbs him how much the woman, in chains, resembles Justice. The chin is the same, the breasts are the same, the left hand is modeled in a familiar gesture. The similarity goes all the way down to the feet, one planted beside a skull, the other resting lightly on the pink reticulation of a conch shell. In the background, Perseus slays a scaled serpent.

Eager to find his companions, Henry turns into the courtyard, looking backward for a final glimpse of the canvas. Just as he steps around the corner into the cool, flagged room, he comes chest to chest with a man hurrying in the opposite direction. It's a wonder that they don't knock each other down. Halfway dazed to begin, Henry registers at first shock, then recognition. It comes in the eyes, nearly equine in their barely contained and superstitious fear. It is Elliot Eckard again. He pauses just long enough to register Henry, draw himself together, and continue quickly on into the first gallery. Henry watches as he scuttles through the room hung with fat schooners and glistening hams.

Grouper Schmidt

The range in our apartment wasn't working correctly. Generally speaking, I didn't complain about things like that going wrong. Other people I knew in the building had much more serious problems: exploded pipes in their walls, collapsed ceilings, once even an electrical fire. I felt fortunate. It was an old but gracious building in a leafy neighborhood in Baltimore. For a pittance, Faith and I had a regular mansion block, with towering ceilings, parquetry, and a formal dining room. The exposures were southern and western; the neighbors were silent. A family trust in fountainy Kansas City owned the building, and that remoteness was reflected in the retrogressive character of the rents. I didn't see the utility in making too much noise. And for three years we had no reason to. It had been like a windfall.

In the fall, things began to change. They fired Betty, the honey-haired manager. In her vague way, she'd maintained equipoise in the building from beneath a halo of cigarette smoke. Next to go was George, the Azorian fixer. Stanley, the sweet porter who lived in a chauffeur's efficiency above the garage and jogged six miles every day, must have feared that he was next. Each morning he vacuumed the lobby's threadbare carpet with gusto then furiously polished the bright brass doors of the elevators. Faith and I lived on the seventh floor.

In early September we went to the beach: five days in a motel room with a kitchen. Faith, who rarely spent money on clothes, spent her time reading nothing but fat fashion magazines. I spent hours in the surf, like someone bugged out, diving compulsively under each thick wave. We were companionable but hardly passionate in our little studio; in fact, we hadn't made love since June. On our last day, the water was huge. A hurricane gathered off the Carolinas. We drove back across the bay in a blinding rain. Baltimore had extensive flooding and blown-down trees. Our building's garage was swamped, and we left our car on the street.

It was on our return from Ocean City that I started noticing the stove. The water took forever to boil; our twice-weekly pot of pasta would begin to dissolve before it cooked through. When the water in the garage had been cleared, and Stanley had gotten most of the fallen debris from the gardens, and otherwise things seemed back to normal, I approached Kelly, our new manager. I explained the problem. It was a new range—that was true—or at least new at our moving in. Perhaps, I thought, there could be some problem in the building's gas lines, a bubble, an occlusion of some sort, something sclerotic. Or maybe the storm had caused it, disrupting the way the gas came in from the street. Other residents might be having a similar problem. I tried to be as nice about it as I could—there was no reason not to be. As I registered my complaint, Stanley stopped his vacuuming and stood by. Bernard, the night manager, whose threadbare distinction matched nicely the grand lobby's faded splendor, folded his *Baltimore Sun*. Kelly filled out the blanks of a work order (itself an innovation). We four talked then about baseball. The Orioles had a chance that year.

The next day there was a knock on the door. A nicotine-wrinkled man with a red toolbox pushed past me. He entered the galley kitchen. A dense orbit of smoke-damage hung around him. His short hair was of ash; he was tall, cylindrical, and lumpen. He twisted the oven's thermostat to 500 then set his box down on the kitchen counter with a gouging crash. From it he dug a round-faced thermometer, which he placed on the oven's middle rack. He slammed shut the door.

"It's the burners, really, that I have the trouble with," I said.

He ignited all four in rapid succession. They hissed with their blue flare.

"They look fine," I said. "I know. But they don't heat the way they used to. That is, they don't seem to provide as much heat somehow." The repairman rubbed an eye. Then, as if it hadn't been enough, he drew both his wrinkled hands down his creased face. He flipped off the burners. With a soiled towel from his toolbox, he removed the hot thermometer from the oven.

"There's nothing wrong with your appliance," he said. "It's fine." That quickly he had the gauge into his toolbox and the lid snapped shut.

"Again—actually—it's not the oven, I've noticed," I said. "It's the range top. I can't get the water to boil the way I need."

He walked to the sink and picked up the saucepan I'd used that morning to boil an egg. He ran two fingers of hot water into it and set it onto a hob. Again he flipped on the gas. He crossed his arms over his chest and leaned back against the counter opposite. We stood there in tense silence. The water formed a skin of bubbles across the bottom of the pan. After the storm, the weather had turned hot again, late September's last gasp. The repairman stared out the kitchen window. The water boiled. He flipped off the gas.

"Looks like it boils to me."

"Well, that's not it, really, is it?" I said. "Two tablespoons of water in a saucepan. That's not the problem I'm having."

"You said it wouldn't boil. It was boiling. Your range works fine."

I'd spent the morning editing a dreary book on interior design. My head ached; I was worn out. "It doesn't work, I told you. And I didn't have you up here to tell me that it did. Because it doesn't." I could feel myself becoming uncontrollably angry. "You can go now," I told him.

"They sent me to repair a broken range," he said. His fitful, Baltimorean accent was getting worse, more sing-songy in his obvious anger. "This range is fine." I could tell that he wanted hit me. He wanted me to do or say one more thing that would justify, in his mind, poking me in the chest. He swung the red toolbox nervously from his right hand. Things were a step from becoming inordinately worse.

"Okay," I said. "My problem. No sweat."

That afternoon I rode the elevator down to the lobby to retrieve my mail. Stanley vacuumed. I stopped at the desk and told Kelly that the repairman was a sham. He hadn't repaired anything. Stanley vacuumed more furiously. Kelly apologized profusely. Perhaps I came off more fiercely than I'd intended.

That night we entertained another couple from the building. They were college friends of Faith's who'd moved to Baltimore from Texas. I made poached flounder and braised lettuce: nothing that required a great deal of heat. When these particular friends first came to town, they'd stayed with us with the idea of finding a house to buy. But they fell in love with our building, and rented on a lower floor. They loved it still, though they had their own problems. Twice they'd had the bathroom in the apartment above flood their ceiling. A bedroom wall had yet, months later, to be repainted. Over dinner, the woman, named Kitty, had this piece of gossip: Betty, the previous manager, had been fired for embezzlement. Ten thousand dollars. She'd been siphoning off petty cash and receipts for years. What had led to her being caught was that in August, she'd slandered a new tenant, a Pakistani, who happened to be a surgical resident at Hopkins Hospital. He'd threatened the Kansas City family trust with a lawsuit. So they started looking into things more closely.

We sat in the solarium eating cheese. I thought of saying something about the incongruity of it all—this fallen building, and Betty the pilfering concierge, brought down by a bit of garden-variety, old Baltimore prejudice. Against a Pakistani surgeon at Hopkins at that. Then it came—all at once. Into a moment of passing silence, there slipped, as if from a ghost, the high-pitched tone of a woman's moaning. It carried on the warm evening air, quite unmistakable and freakishly acoustical. Our nearest neighbor, whose bedroom window abutted our kitchen wall, had a woman over. We'd never before heard even a footfall in the year that we'd known him to be there.

Kitty took it all without the least bit of humor. Her husband looked green. She started to say something, and the noises grew louder. Faith got up. She disappeared into the dining room, its table crowded with breadcrumbs and plates, then into the kitchen. I heard the window close. On her way back into the solarium, she stopped and tuned the radio to the jazz program. We returned to talking. Jerry was a doctor, too, at the University of Maryland. He knew the Pakistani surgeon in question. We carried on as if nothing had happened, though I continued to consider it. It was uncanny, really, the way her voice had carried. Amidst a quiet vibraphone solo, I thought that I heard her again, but the noises never really broke through. The cheese finished, our guests rode the elevator home.

The next night, I decided at the last minute that I couldn't bear going to the symphony. Faith's parents had given us the tickets. It was too late to do anything else with them, and if we let them go to waste, there'd be hell to pay from her mother. Faith cross-questioned me about it, wanting to know what was "really wrong." *Christ already*, I said. I put on a jacket and we went. What was I going to say? That I felt clinically insane?

At the intermission I stood in line for a drink. It was a long line that stretched into the lobby. The febrile yellow light hurt my eyes. Everyone around me—the people in line ahead of me, those milling aimlessly behind—all looked miserable as well. They were a singularly ugly crowd. I thought of my neighbor and his wild date the night before. They weren't at this moment at Meyerhoff Hall, waiting eagerly to hear something riveting by Poulenc. Oh, to be in love. To be just *dating*. To have a life in three dimensions.

We suffered through the Poulenc. The ride home passed in silence. In the elevator, Faith stood close to the polished doors, as if the car were crowded. Stanley's polished brass reflected the set of her mouth. The doors opened. I waited for a moment in the elevator, my finger upon the < > button. I followed her down the long, carpeted hall, past the louvered door of our neighbor. They were together, in the living room, it sounded like, on a couch, or the floor maybe. Her slow moans came echoed the length of the cavernous hall. I reached Faith at our door, where she stood, crying and pawing through her small bag for her keys. She hadn't brought them. I took mine from my pocket and opened the door.

We didn't speak for two days. I listened a lot to our neighbor. Each morning after getting the papers I set the coffee water to its interminable boil, opened the kitchen window, and sat on the wooden stool beside it. And each morning, at twenty of seven or so—when his alarm sounded, I supposed—it began. I could hear them, or, rather—I could hear *her*—clearly across the short divide that separated our apartments. It was as if I could reach out and touch her. Our neighbor was Russian, I'd gathered from his name and the heavy accent that I'd heard the two or three times he'd grunted hello. He was a physician, or so I assumed. He had the obligatory "Dr." scribbled before his name on the cards in the apartment door and the lobby mailbox, and twice I'd seen him in the corridor wearing leek-green scrubs. Certainly, their lovemaking had a little of the Cossack to it. Generally the coupling lasted until my water boiled. I wondered if I was as obvious to them, sitting quietly on my stool, idly turning the pages of my morning paper, as they were to me.

Faith flew to Kentucky on business. The day that she left, sometime a little before noon, there came a light knock on the door. Light streamed in through the windows of the solarium and dining room, casting bright, reticulated boxes of gold on the polished parquetry. It struck me how quiet the apartment, the building, even the street below, was at that moment. I answered the door. It was another repairman. But this one couldn't have been more different from the first. He'd been coached, it seemed, because he treated me gingerly. Rather than a uniform, he wore tidy, casual clothes—slacks and a golf shirt. His toolbox, which he set gently on the floor, was brushed steel.

"Your stove's on the fritz, I believe?" he said with a smile. He removed his pressed barracuda jacket. I offered to take it for him. "I can leave it here," he said, draping it gently over the back of a dining-room chair.

He stood before the range like a consulting physician. He was a big, robust man in his mid-fifties, I guessed. Gently he twisted the oven's controlling knob to 500. One by one he lit the burners.

"They tell me you're a gourmet chef," he said as he adjusted each burner's control.

"Of course not," I said. "I just cook." I was embarrassed that my pretense was common knowledge in the lobby.

"My wife loves to cook," he said. "She can do it by touch. By that I mean, we'll eat out and she can identify what we're eating, the type of fish or meat, the spices, what exactly has gone into the sauce. Then she can recreate it exactly as it was, better sometimes. I have a few things I cook. I have my 'dishes' I guess you'd say." He took a thermometer from his open toolbox and set it carefully upon the center rack in the oven. Gently closing the door, he rested a hand on the countertop. "We'll give it a minute. Do you eat out much? Do you know the Castillian?"

In those days, the best restaurant in Baltimore was a Spanish place in a cellar in Mount Vernon. I said that I did, of course.

"My wife and I go once a month. Every month, even the summer. We both love it. I have my own dish there. It's grouper, but rather than they way they do it usually, I get it with the chef's champagne sauce. That is, my version of his sauce—with shrimp. I have it every time. Grouper Schmidt, they call it. Schmidt being me: Jim Schmidt. Ask for it sometime; you'll see."

He had such a confident way about him, and the story was sufficiently offbeat—an appliance repairman a regular at Baltimore's best restaurant—as to be utterly plausible.

"Does your wife make it?" I asked. "Has she figured it out?"

He opened the oven and checked the thermostat—he studied it.

"She never . . . Well, it's my dish," he said, smiling warmly. "She's never been great with the champagne sauce. My daughter loved it, too. It was a thing that the two of us shared. You see, her husband . . . Are you at Hopkins?"

It was a natural question: The university was across the street. Like the slandered Pakistani surgeon, a lot of Hopkins people lived in the building. I told him that Faith was, in administration at the hospital.

"My son-in-law did his residency there. That's where they met. My daughter was getting her master's at Hygiene."

I made the obligatory acknowledgment of the achievement. It was a sort of Baltimore ritual, the obeisant recognition of Hopkins' supersuperiority.

"They got married when he finished his residency. Moved out to Colorado. He got this terrific job in a practice in Colorado Springs. He was a pediatric cardiologist. Top guy."

I told him that I knew about Colorado Springs.

"Terrific, beautiful place," he said. "Of course, we didn't love her being so far from home, but it was perfect for them. You know: biking, hiking, all that. The mountains. Both of them outdoorsy. And his practice took right off, you know. Saving blue babies and what not. He was in with five other guys, Colorado Springs was booming, he had this great job. But also he was doing some new stuff, important stuff. He even saved the governor's daughter. Oh, really. It was a big thing. They loved him out there."

Once again he opened the door to the oven and studied the thermostat. "Then one day, three years ago: boom. My daughter. She woke up one morning feeling sick. Couldn't shake it. Needless to say, they looked into it right away. Cancer."

For the second time that morning I was struck by the apartment's eerie silence, the bright light in lozenges on the parquet and carpets, the dust motes dancing like champagne bubbles in the stalactites of light, the scent of autumn hovering just outside the screen. Schmidt opened the oven, checked his thermostat, and then removed it with a pair of metal tongs. He dropped the hot thermostat into his toolbox and turned the oven off.

"We brought her back to Hopkins, of course. Her husband knew all the big stars in oncology over there. They all worked on her. But there was nothing they could do. It was one of those things. She just went so quickly. She was dead in four months."

I lifted up my right hand as if to do something with it, then let it drop. "I'm so sorry," I said.

He gave a little nod. "Thanks," he said. "My son-in-law just couldn't go back to Colorado. He sold his share in the practice. They couldn't believe he was leaving. The governor, even, called him on the phone and begged him to stay. He came back to Baltimore. I guess he just feels more comfortable here. He works over at Good Sam now, doing emergency room stuff. It's a bit of a letdown, you know, after all the research and celebrity, I guess. He still goes to her grave every day. Rain, cold, snow, you name it. Every day."

Schmidt smiled, and then he started to cry. He stood with his arms at his side and tears ran down his cheeks. He didn't make a sound, his shoulders did not heave, he just cried.

I started to cry, too. I put my arms around him. Schmidt was taller than I was, but I put my arms around him. After a second, he put his arms around me. I could smell his cologne and the laundry detergent scent in his shirt. We let go of each other, looked away, and wiped our eyes.

"Well," he said. "Try it the next time you go. Ask for the Grouper Schmidt." He closed up his toolbox and snapped its chrome buckles shut. "As for this thing," he nodded to the stove. "As far as I can measure, it's going. But between you, me, and the wall, it's not a great stove, even new. Probably never worked that well. Still, there could be a problem in the line, making it worse. It happens in these old buildings. Your next step would be to get a plumber in here. Your pressure might be off, or it might be low for the entire building. He'd check first the foot-pounds coming in at the street and then at your floor. But that is, as I said, plumbing." He lifted his box and got his barracuda jacket off the back of the chair in the dining room. He smiled.

"Grouper Schmidt," I said to him at the door.

"Grouper Schmidt," he said, patting me on the shoulder. "Keep on cooking."

Faith returned from Kentucky the next afternoon. She seemed refreshed, or at least, reset. That night I made dinner—some softshells with parsley and capers. After we'd eaten and cleaned up, we sat down to read in the living room. Without any sort of preamble—that was her way with bad news—she announced that she had taken a job in Lexington. The business trip had been in reality an interview. The position had come up suddenly and a colleague in Baltimore had recommended her for it. The job represented a significant promotion for her. She liked the people she met and found the hospital to be a lively place. The meetings went well; they offered her the position. She accepted.

I got up from the sofa. My keys and my money were in my pocket already. I left the apartment as if I was walking only into the next room. The hallway was silent; the elevator came immediately. In the hushed lobby, Bernard sat beneath the manager's sign, reading his *Baltimore Sun*. Outside the dark evening was cool and still and there was the smell of wood smoke in the air. I walked along the sidewalk. Pebbles of blue tempered glass lay at the curb. I went down the block, past the French restaurant on the corner with its yellow windows and empty bar. I crossed a small ravine and was on the campus of Hopkins. I wandered its paths, past the undergraduates in ones and twos, beneath the unshaded windows of the dormitories, between the dark classroom buildings, the humming labs, the windowless blocks. I must have walked behind a dining hall: The cool air warmed suddenly with a blowing exhaust of confused aromas. At the school's stadium some rain began to fall. A lone jogger hurried along the red composite oval. I recognized him: He was Faith's college friend, the doctor who lived in our building. For half a circuit I stood and watched him plodding gracelessly through the now pouring rain. With a jet engine's whoosh of sound, the rain began falling even harder, turning into a silver veil. I turned home. By the time I reached the lobby, water was running down the middle of the street.

Upstairs, Faith's trench coat lay across a chair inside the door, lightly flecked with rain.

"I came to look for you," she said. Outside, the storm smeared the windows.

That weekend the Orioles played for the division in Toronto. They lost. I forget who went on to win the Series that year; maybe it was Toronto. Poor Stanley, who'd kept his job after all, had followed the O's closely to the end. With their elimination, he couldn't hide his disappointment.

After three terrible days of fighting we agreed to a truce. We agreed to live peaceably and without further discussion until the fourth of December, the day she had scheduled to move south. And in fact, we did. We got along nicely. We had quite a pleasant Thanksgiving—the best we'd ever spent together. It was romantic, even. We ate ossetra caviar off a set of bone spoons that she'd bought me once at Gump's while on a business trip. I roasted game hens in an orange sauce. We drank Pol Roger rosé and went to bed early.

On Monday, I flew to Morocco. I took the once weekly from Dulles. An old friend who designed software was going there to do work for the king. He brought me along, he said, because it looked bad, his going alone. But it would look worse taking any of the people who actually worked for him. It was a small office. We shared a large suite in a marble-tiled hotel in Rabat. Virtually upon landing I came down with a terrible cold and spent most of the week in the hotel. The suite had a remarkable view across the Bu-Regreg River. At its mouth, where the river met the sea, there was an ancient Muslim cemetery. The sun hung at an impossibly low angle, and the whitewashed sepulchers cast their rounded blue shadows across the cemetery's low wall and onto the deserted beach. I spent most of my time in an armchair in front of the window, wrapped in towels and staring at the marvelous and frightening view.

I returned to Baltimore to find my Russian neighbor and his girlfriend sitting silently in the middle of the lobby. She looked much the way I had imagined her—pale, with long black hair and lips that were sensual to the point of being untamed. They were waiting for a hired car. They wore their heavy coats—his shearling and hers edged in fur—and were circled by luggage. She returned my look almost lasciviously. It was as if she didn't speak English—or that no English could convey her animal meaning. Her green eyes were otherworldly. The Russians were moving, and I never saw them again.

I got my mail from Bernard, then waited at the polished brass doors of the elevator. The seventh floor was gloomy and silent. I walked down the long corridor. When I opened my door, for one moment the apartment looked as if Faith hadn't gone.

The furniture remained in its usual places; the walls had no ghost marks from frames removed. The late afternoon's light still blanched the parquetry, revealing the flaws in the tiles, spreading like crackle, from seventy years of tenants' shuffle.

It was only in the study that her absence, like a well-hidden fraud, began to announce itself. The contents of an entire side of the room had disappeared, leaving only stray paper clips, a lone penny, the cap from a film canister, and a few rubber bands on the floor. In the bedroom, the devastation was as obvious and complete as the touchdown of a twister. Gone was the rug, the mirrors, a framed photograph of Faith as a little girl in Georgia. The bed-clothes were from my bachelor days; a wool blanket had replaced the fluffy duvet. There were half as many pillows. Her dresser was gone, shockingly enlarging the room and leaving an unmistakable sense of despair. I put down my bags and went to the kitchen. Opening the window, I could hear the painters laughing as they worked in the apartment next door.

A few years later I found myself at the Castillian, the Spanish restaurant where Jim Schmidt had told me to order the fish. It was the seventieth birthday of my fiancée's father. We were a big group, eighteen people at least. I sat at one corner of the long table. I remember at the time feeling oddly outside of it all—this group that was soon to become my extended clan. A waiter delivered two big trays of garlic shrimp. A second followed with pitchers of sangria. When he set one of the jugs at my end of the long table, I signaled to him. He bent over and I asked if they still had the Grouper Schmidt. He paused, then made me repeat the name, twice. Then he had me describe it. Finally he gave me one of those splendid looks of Iberian exasperation. He puffed cheeks, rolled his eyes, and grasped with his fingertips at nothing.

I have a photograph somewhere of that dinner. It amuses my wife that I don't like to talk about what she calls my "first marriage." I have a friend who lives now in the old building. He tells me that Stanley works there still, still vacuuming the lobby's faded carpet every day. I feel that I, too, in some horrible way, have not changed much since that time.

Personals

Me: three years old, living at the middle of a short street edging the Highline Canal.

You: precocious playmate who on hot afternoons shows me her privates.

Me: towhead in a sailor suit with blood pouring down his forehead. Three stitches needed.

You: girl from opposite end of street, whom I frequently visit in mornings because parents walk around the house naked while dressing for work. This presents unrivaled opportunities for studying your mother's secondary sexual characteristics. You have mastered the art of peeing like a boy, which you demonstrate when requested. One morning following dressing of parents, you concoct a wagon ride whereby I am to be pulled down a steep cement driveway until the moment you turn onto the sidewalk to prevent entry into the forbidden street. On dry run, the plan looks viable. With my added weight to the little red wagon, however, no amount of pulling on the black metal yoke will halt my forward motion. I am catapulted into the gutter. Blood flows copiously, into my eyes, even. You lead me home and show me to my mother. She calls you a "stupid little girl."

Me: a child of seven, eating dinner in a restaurant in Mazatlan. It is the spring of 1970.

You: a beautiful dark-haired woman at the next table, dining with two handsome men. You drink wine from a *jarra*, tilting your head back, opening your mouth wide, showing two brilliantly white rows of teeth, a sensual tongue. Your tanned arms are bare; on your left you wear a large silver cuff, sandcast with scrollwork.

Me: a student in the third grade at Fallis Elementary.

You: a girl called Fleurette, with dark hair and fair skin, who transfers into my class halfway through the year. In May, I move with my family to a different neighborhood, though I bump into you once, perhaps a year later, on the ground floor of a department store. I have with you the very first moments of physical yearning, the knowledge of measurable arousal.

Me: a high school student backpacking with a friend through Switzerland, hut sleeping, hash smoking, living off chocolate, sweet local wine, and a flank of dried meat purchased expectantly in Brig.

You: a girl wearing a blue Speedo who pulls on a swimming cap and goggles, strolls down the lawn of the hostel in which we all stay, and dives from a dock into Lake Thurn.

> In Fullensee she swam toward me
> Backstroke, breaststroke, crawl.

Me: just graduated from college, living in San Francisco alone, at my first job, desperate and lonely, knowing only an aunt and uncle in Marin County and a disreputable cousin in insurance adjusting. Each week's highlight and sole excursion is Thursday evenings at the old San Francisco Museum of Modern Art, on two upper floors at the War Memorial.

You: tall, slim, we make eye contact before the three Diebenkorns and spend the rest of the evening trading eye traffic as we wonder through the adjoining rooms. We meet there for three weeks running, always at the same time. We never speak.

Me: mid-twenties, sandy hair, just returning from a six-month job in North Africa.

You: an Irish woman working at a German resort for the summer, traveling home for vacation. You sing blues standards at the bar, eat with me in the Romerberg through an impossibly long twilight, then kiss me in the shadows of a church. You sleep beside me in a room provided by Lufthansa for a missed flight, though pointedly not with me: *I couldn't sleep with you without feeling quite the slut.* When you leave in the morning you say: "You're a strange man: I'll remember you always."

Me: seated at the edge of a naked-dancing runway in Glendale, Colorado.

You: the prettiest girl there, wearing a black fedora, a white smoking jacket, and nothing more. The barker calls you Tina from New York City, but when you crouch upon your black high heels before me to collect your tip you cry: "I went to elementary school with you!" It is Fleurette, dancing at this bar and traveling in the entourage of a rock band when she isn't working.

Me: turning the corner of Charles Street onto Chestnut Avenue.

You: an attractive woman driving a silver Mercedes-Benz station wagon. Your dark hair is up, held in place by a chopstick.

Me: ABC.

You: the bottom quark, which, in decay, produces an asymmetrically large amount of antimatter, thus being the possible cause of the strange fact that there is far more antimatter in the universe than matter.

Me: driving on I-95, somewhere in South Carolina.

You: a black coupe that appears in my rearview mirror, shimmery in the humid, laurenced air above the black ribbon of interstate. You are driving well over ninety. I see you as you appear over a hill in the rolling landscape. You gain upon me steadily, quickly. When you pass, I catch a glimpse of you: slim, dark hair, large black sunglasses, a black knit dress, no luggage, no map, merely a single-minded focus on gobbling the road ahead.

Me: sincere, refined, warm, seeking companionship and an interest in music, museums, and the arts.

You: the gravistar, a hypothetical alternative to the black hole. Rather than an infinitely small point in space-time, the gravistar represents the final steady state of a collapsed star. Unlike the black hole, which rests on the notion of an event horizon, the gravistar is understood to have volume, specifically, a spherical shell of ultimately hard, incredibly thin material that is black. All matter drawn toward it is pinged outward. Inside is a homogenous vacuum that might contain its own matter. Indeed, our entire universe may be contained within some unimaginably large gravistar, itself part of another universe beyond our comprehension.

Me: lonely, bored, alone. Dejected, disconsolate, depressed. Objectionable. Angry, hurt, cheated. Suspicious, longing, jealous. Ruined. Drinking an eleven-thirty morning martini at the bar of Tadich's, after a late, late, bibulous business dinner the night before. Embarrassed. Isolate, precipitate, contrariwise. Athwart, asunder, high-centered. Effectively negated, associatively disordered, undesired weight loss, interrupted sleep, unruly thoughts of self-cessation. Decompensating. Ideating. Dialogically impaired.

You: the first Irish girl, at the bar, trying desperately to figure fifty-five cents in change. On your holiday, your first visit to the States. You're seeing your brother who has a home-renovation job in the Richmond. So different here, so expensive, you say. The people are not at all friendly. Superficial, self-absorbed, materialistic, status-conscious. You see little meaningful exchange. The San Franciscans you've met are fixated on expensive restaurants and their trendy cars. In Ireland, everyone's on the dole, in the same boat, as it were. A party is pitching in on a bottle and spending the night in one place or another, talking and playing guitar. And: Which is the nickel? And: Why is it *bigger* than the dime? *Why?*

Me: you.
You: you.

Me: when we meet again in Philadelphia, following a year apart. A year cloudy to opaque, a year of misty seances, interdigitating dreams, missed leads. We visit Rittenhouse Square: the apartment building where your father lives. "Hi, Jeff," I say upon entering, a bit too loudly. *Friday, Saturday, Sunday.* We walk across the Thirty-second Street bridge. The boathouses are strung with Christmas lights. We eat prelapsarian dinners and spend evenings in your bedroom on Pine Street. In the mornings we shower together. The smell of floor wax, radiator heat, and boxwood brushed in passing hangs in the hallways of your shared brownstone. Spring. An Easter service on the Mainline with your mother and a sister: the purple, the pageant, the brass band, and the lawn pocked with onion grass. Afterward, back in Center City, we wander through Society Hill.
    You: I'll see you another year. I'll see you again.
    Returning home, I see Solitude from the train.

Snowflake

Lara and Jay Carpenter lived in a small house at the end of Carberry Lane, where it met Cricket Hill Road. On the plats, the area was called Cricket Hill Heights, to distinguish it from Cricket Hill proper, across Roland Run and the commuter rail tracks, where the much bigger houses were. After taking their daughter, Jennifer, to the St. Stephen's Christmas Eve service, held at three, they walked back down the hill. St. Stephen's was at the top of Carberry Lane, where it met Weatherly Avenue, Cricket Hill's thoroughfare. They pushed Jennifer in her stroller. It was unseasonably warm for December, and the golden light of the late afternoon ran down the sloping lawns of Cricket Hill, daubing their dormant beds with rich sienna and umber. Cricket Hill affected a country look rather than a suburban one: Witch's broom and tangled forsythia marked property lines. The fence posts were wound with one vine or another, and lightning strikes of dormant rosebushes flashed through the weathered pickets.

Halfway down the lane was Harry Bailey's house. Bailey had made tens of millions on television stations, and he was assumed by most to be the street's wealthiest resident. But true intelligence on Carberry Lane, and in all of Cricket Hill, was hard to come by.

There were vaster fortunes still in the village, families whose tap-roots reached back to some boom sounded and forgotten already, long before Alexander Bell, let alone the wireless. These families rested like old game behind the overgrown fences, driving dented station wagons down long rutted drives. Jay Carpenter himself fig-ured that the richest on Carberry Lane was probably Grenville VanDenberg, friendly and ineffectual, who drove a sun-faded German sedan with rusting rocker panels and lived with his three daughters in a rambling house opposite the Baileys. He served on every museum board in town and spent, from what Jay gathered on their occasional conversations in the lane, more than half the year in Paris.

Next after the Baileys came the Kincaids. Dan and Renée Kin-caid came to Baltimore from Atlanta and had an infant son named Tilghman. Dan Kincaid was in his yard, wrestling with a spool of lights, and Jay and Lara stopped to talk with him. Every time the two couples spoke, they mentioned their desire to get together for dinner. After a moment, Lara pushed on: It was getting dark, and the baby had not worn a heavy jacket to the service. Jay stayed a moment longer, and he and Dan stood talking until the porch light came on and Renée appeared with a smile and a wave from behind the storm door. Dan and Jay finished their conversation, wished one another a Merry Christmas, and Jay continued on in a festive spirit down the long-shadowed lane.

Near the bottom of Carberry Lane, a hedge of young maple trees separated Jay's house from his neighbor's. As Jay came to it, on the empty and now nearly dark street, he passed a teenager who wore a sweatshirt and hood. Jay and Lara had lived in the city be-fore moving up to Cricket Hill, and Jay still had certain urban in-stincts. He didn't recognize the boy; but for the three VanDenberg girls, no other teens lived on the lane. The boy seemed to shudder ever so slightly upon seeing Jay, a self-conscious gesture that made Jay even more suspicious. Because the Carpenters lived at the end of Carberry, where it met Cricket Hill Road, there was little reason for him to be walking that way. Across the road lay nothing but the commuter tracks. Jay looked after him while he passed and wondered.

His suspicions were confirmed as he came up his walk—there was something on their front step. On closer inspection, he found that it was a large wicker gift basket, filled with cookies, some fruit, foil-wrapped bread, and chocolates, all nested in a bed of excelsior. A cut-paper snowflake, awkwardly made but sincere, hung from the handle. Lara parted the curtain and then pulled open the door as Jay examined the contents of the basket. She had Jennifer on her hip.

"God," she said. "We've been waiting for you to come. What is it?"

Jay poked in the excelsior: He found a chocolate orange—the kind opened with a crack—some loose almonds and walnuts, a fruit pudding, and three unmarked glass vials to which had been attached a note in a woman's hand that read "Bubbles!"

"Come in," Lara said. "I was reading to Jennifer when I heard someone on the steps. They knocked."

"A teenager, wearing a sweatshirt?"

"I didn't see. He was gone by the time I looked. What *is* it? You know how these things freak me out."

"I passed him in the street. He looked like a neighborhood kid; maybe from over on Weatherly or Collington." Among the green paper shavings and wrapped packets, there was a sheet of paper, folded twice. *Surprise!!!* it read. Beneath there was a long story, printed out on someone's home computer. It was, loosely, the legend of St. Nicholas—a terrible storm, starvation in a remote Norse village, a kindly farmer who risked all to deliver a load of wheat by a team of reindeer. Thus, December sixth was St. Nicholas's Day, celebrated by the delivery of holiday baskets between friends. The rules were simple. Receive a basket, then tape the homemade snowflake on one's door. Prepare a new basket, cut a new snowflake, and deliver it to someone on the street without a snowflake already. "Every door on the lane should have a snowflake by Christmas!" the note concluded.

Jay put the basket down on the table inside the door and looked at his watch. It was five minutes of five, Christmas Eve. He tried to think if he'd seen any other snowflakes on the lane. In any event, it was hopeless: One could never pull together a basket so late in the day on Christmas Eve. In other words, whether or not they were the first, the Carpenters were certainly last, and the chain of baskets would end for the year there, at number forty-nine.

The following morning, Christmas Day, the basket remained on the table in the entry. They arrayed Jennifer's gifts and stuffed the stockings. Jay ate half the cookies and part of the carrot, to show that Santa had visited. When their daughter woke, they opened her presents, she played in the wrapping, and then fell back to sleep by ten. In the afternoon, Lara's parents and an aunt and uncle came to the house for an early meal. That quickly, the day was done.

Early the next morning, Boxing Day, they took Jennifer for her usual stroll up the lane. The weather had turned seasonable, and hoarfrost glistened like filigree on the lawns and cars that sat parked, still with the holiday, in the bright morning light along the lane and drives. Now looking consciously, they saw the snowflakes everywhere—some large, others goofily small—in the front door of every house in the lane but two. In one of the flakeless houses lived a very old woman with an around-the-clock nurse. The other was that of a couple who'd left for Florida in mid-November. Even the Kincaids' house had one. All this played heavily on Jay's insecurities: Cricket Hill was a tribal place, where everyone seemed to have known each other's families since the dawn of man. The Carpenters' house was the smallest on the lane, and had been, for a number of years before they bought it, a rental. Jay worried that, although he had done a great deal of improvement, people might think it was a rental still. So the idea that he'd gotten his basket *after* the newer family on the block, the Kincaids, whose house was only slightly bigger, after all, though equipped with a startling new kitchen addition, reawakened certain anxieties that he'd never entirely quieted. If nothing else, he thought he'd have some sort of seniority.

Neither he nor Lara could understand how they'd not noticed the snowflakes in the windows, especially as they walked up and down the street every day. And yet there they were. The Kincaids had one of the larger ones, even. As they continued on their walk, Renée Kincaid, dressed in workout clothes and driving her husband's car, pulled up.

"Did *you* give us the basket?" Jay asked her.

Renée laughed as she unstrapped baby Tilghman from his safety seat. "No, Jay, I did not. I wish I would have. I meant to pass mine on, I really did. I woke up at four in the morning thinking, 'Oh, that damn basket.' But I had cookies for the playgroup Tilghman is in, and my book club was having a gift exchange, and between getting stuff up to Dan's family in Boston and to my brothers and sisters, and with all that, I just didn't do it. Now I feel awful. I must have broken the chain."

Jay and Lara walked on up to St. Stephen's playground, where they set Jennifer in the baby swing. Obviously, Renée Kincaid *hadn't* broken the chain. But if she had had the basket for a week and never passed it on, how was it then that another basket made it to their house? They speculated on the possible suspects. Jay clung to the notion that it was Grenville VanDenberg. He was an organizer and community minded. At Easter there'd been a big egg hunt in his yard and a parade on the Fourth of July. It made sense that he would begin the Christmas baskets, then see the program through to completion when it faltered.

"We should invite the Kincaids for dinner on New Year's Eve," Jay said. He was pushing Jennifer. Already they had invited Ned and Erin Stoltz, a couple whose daughter had been in Jennifer's Mommy-and-Me. "They're new to Baltimore. It's possible that they don't have anywhere to go."

Lara shrugged. It appeared that she was thinking still about the basket. "I guess," she said.

New Year's Eve came, and the Kincaids, who had gladly accepted Lara's invitation, arrived at seven. Ned and Erin came up the walk behind them. In his hands Ned carried an expensive bottle of wine, along with some champagne, the label of which Jay saw Dan Kincaid sneak a peek at as Ned held it. Amid the bustle of meeting and removing coats, Jay realized with embarrassment that he'd never moved the St. Nicholas basket.

"Renée," he said again, "are you sure you didn't give this to us?"

Renée, who was blonde and slim and wore a velvet headband, looked aghast. It seemed to Jay that she and her husband moved closer together.

"What is it?" asked Ned, poking in the excelsior with an exploratory pinkie.

Dan Kincaid laughed loudly. "That's the basket *we* sent," he said. "Isn't it, babe? The one we gave to the Baileys?"

"I think it is," Renée said, bending over to look at the rather sad snowflake dangling from the basket's handle. "You know, it is!"

Lara couldn't help but give her husband a nervous glance. The Baileys, with the television fortune, lived across the lane from the Kincaids. The young evening felt as fragile as fresh ice on a pond.

"Big mystery," Jay said, trying to shuffle his guests into the living room. "You're supposed to pass it on," he explained to Ned and Erin. "Something Scandinavian about St. Nick and a basket of wheat."

Everyone was seated at last.

The fire in the hearth only limped along, smoking, and the music was the bland female vocals that Lara listened to on her treadmill. The bowl of guacamole was still frozen, and Jay, momentarily stunned by the Kincaids' admission, failed to offer anyone a drink. Then Lara brought out some smoked Scottish salmon that she'd bought at the village market. Jay thought to pour wine, and the mood revived somewhat. Except that the smoked salmon was a failure—only Ned Stoltz ate three slices quickly before his wife stilled him with an accusatory glance—and the fire had sputtered out. Lara called the guests to the table. They started with a salad of baby greens, which, Jay noticed, neither Dan nor Renée made much of an effort at. Lemon chicken was usually Lara's best dish, but this time it came to the table acidic and dry. The pasta she served with it was cold. Mainly, they drank the wine.

The question of the Christmas baskets came up again.

"Did everybody get one?" Ned asked, "or was it just some families, or what?"

"What was in the little vials?" Lara asked Renée. "I thought it was poison." Lara wasn't used to drinking wine. Her cheeks were flushed and her tongue a little thick. "What was that poison they put in the Tokyo subway?" she said to the table at large.

"Sarin," Ned said. "Furlong Bong or Fung-shui Gong or something. Japanese revolutionaries, I think. Religious wackos."

"It was bubblebath, I think we decided," Jay said.

"Bubblebath," Renée said quietly, almost into her napkin as she brought it to her mouth.

"What happens if you put sarin in your bath, I wonder?" Jay asked.

"What happens if you put a toaster in your bath?" Ned said. He as well was getting flushed from the wine.

Lara got up a little unsteadily and went to the kitchen to prepare the dessert, a warm chocolate cake. The centers were meant to be runny with dark chocolate, but they came to the table nearly gelatinous. Jay opened the bottle of champagne he'd been chilling, thinking that he'd save Erin and Ned's much better bottle for the stroke of twelve. But Erin had been falling asleep in her place since before the dessert, and both Dan and Renée barely sipped a toast from theirs. There wasn't any demand for a second bottle.

At ten past the New Year, Dan and Renée rose from the table. They'd been invited to a party in the city. They didn't mind not being there for the stroke of twelve, but afterward there was going to be dancing. Erin was happy to go as well, and she and her husband slipped out ahead of the Kincaids.

"We've got to get you over sometime," Renée told Lara as they stood together at the door. Fireworks could be heard popping in the distance. The lights that Jay had strung along his picket fence twinkled in the cold. "I am going to call you and we'll pick a date."

The next morning early Jay retrieved the Christmas basket from the table in the hall. He threw away the excelsior and food and hung the empty basket from a rafter in the basement.

The rest of winter went by, and then the spring. Jay and Lara saw the Kincaids in the lane, much as they had before, though the promised invitation to dinner was never forthcoming. In March, a large blue-and-white realtor's sign appeared in the Kincaids' yard. The house was on the market. It sold in one day, and the Kincaids were gone as quickly as they had arrived.

Night

Night; he wakes and it is night and he squeezes himself orange juice, makes coffee, and eats a bowl of cereal. It is night. He showers and shaves and combs his hair and dresses: dark gabardine trousers, blue shirt, red silk tie, sports jacket, and Italian shoes. He goes to his office and works until night falls upon night. Night; he dreams vivid dreams—dreams more vivid than life: encounters in a stairwell, a passing elevator, someone waving from the end of a corridor. He wakes as night spreads upon night. Night; one night he awakens to find himself levitating from his bed. He floats out the bedroom window—he floats upon his back across the dark neighborhood, deathly quiet below. Night; dreams; a decorated cake, its multitudinous candles waver in a ghostly, silent breeze. All around it sit bubbling flutes of champagne. The bubbles die. The candles flicker out. Night dawns upon night, becoming darker still. He wakes to sleep and lies upon his bed.

After much quiet searching, he finds it, that which, without knowing it, he has been looking for all along. There is a giant switch in his chest, like the wall control for a light. With the gentlest of gestures, he turns it off. Darkness falls over night.

She Is the Mother of the Cat

He parks in the market's small lot. A black sedan idles in the grocery pick-up lane. There isn't a box boy around, and a pretty middle-aged woman struggles to lift three paper sacks of groceries into the sedan's voluminous open trunk. She wears a black knit dress with a small gold buckle at the waist, black stockings, and black shoes. As he passes, she fixes her eye intently on him. Perhaps he has embarrassed her by watching her struggle. She continues staring at him as she enters the back of the car. As he passes by he glances toward the car's driver, expecting to see a chauffeur. It's not common to see a chauffeur at this particular market; however, located as it is between three different exclusive enclaves, it's not unheard of, either. Instead of the expected billed cap, there is a young woman behind the wheel, a young woman also nicely dressed and blonde, who resembles the older woman in a close way. Mother and daughter. He smiles to her in surprise; he has misread the situation. He continues along the breezeway and enters the market. It is the Friday after Thanksgiving and the store has the usual postholiday air of mystery and surfeit about it. He's entertaining that night and lingers in the produce and bakery, deciding what to prepare. Three different acquaintances stop him in the aisles to air their disappointment with the evening before. "Every happy family is the same," the last, a small man in horn-rimmed glasses, says. "Every unhappy family is, also, *the same.*"

He checks out, his groceries compactly in three sacks.

In the market's breezeway he is surprised to find the large black sedan idling there still. He smiles in the driver's direction. Why haven't they left already? It's late afternoon and there's the smell of wood smoke in the air. Fallen maple leaves stir across the sloping car lot. A horn sounds. He pauses, then reaches into the cart for his bags. The young woman, the driver of the black sedan, honks again, this time twice. He looks up at her. She is flashing him the finger. They make eye contact, and she holds the emphatic flip-off before him, pumping her hand even, it seems to him. The mother stares over her daughter's right shoulder. She can see, certainly, the gesture. His three heavy grocery bags dangle at his side, but he continues to smile, though he can't see what's funny anymore. He's just confused. She flashes him the finger a second time, quickly, but doesn't drop her hard gaze. He walks back up the breezeway, passing, as he must, her closed window. He carries his bags and studies her warily: early twenties, honey-colored hair, carefully combed, a black knit dress, and dark anger in her eyes. "Yes, *you,*" she mouths through the greenish glass as he passes her. And she flips him off again.

Alias

He decides to contact all the people he has lost touch with, alienated, dropped, pissed off, or cheated in a romantic way. Of course, some don't make the list, people he cut off for, in his mind, just causes: cheats themselves, thieves, liars, and functional sociopaths into whose orbit he had drifted, sometimes reluctantly, at other times with mistaken enthusiasm. They were—the justified cases— in the minority. The vast majority of those names on the list in his mind were victims of his own insensitivity, carelessness, and regularly selfish behavior. Most had been for some time, at least, good friends—dinner companions, trip pals, drinking buddies, lovers, and close confidants. When he trusted a person, he opened up easily. Sometimes he had broken with these people in a mistaken fit of righteousness. In other cases, the reasons were little more than unfortunate convergences: missed calls, fleeing moves to different cities, shifted allegiances, bar-talk gone sour, and morning boredom. Sometimes it was simply the weariness that comes too often with friends who are made of necessity rather than choice.

For two days he works at his project: writing, calling, e-mailing, faxing, instant-messaging, or Googling when he can't locate the person either in his address book or from calling information in the city where he last remembered him or her. It goes on for a week, then two, then a month. Some people pick up on the first ring. Others require days of sleuthing. He begins keeping a log, in an old ledger book. He learns a great deal. Very much has gone on in the years he's lost touch. There've been marriages, children, deaths, some accidental, one a suicide, job promotions, changes, losses, affairs, divorces, remarriages, happy solitude, businesses started, bought, sold, cratered, and revivified. There have been relocations, dislocations, emigrations, aliyah, conversions, apostasies, Ph.D.s, long-term illnesses suddenly cured, undiagnosed conditions arrived at in a heartbeat. There have been roots and uprootings, comings-out and goings-in, rediscoveries, mysterious disappearances, psychic transferences, unbalances, and transgressions aplenty. There was even a sex change. The capacity of his old ledger gets outstripped; he turns to a laptop computer. This device works to track his research at first, but as it grows to include thousands of names, as well as the meticulous documentation of their lives, even the latest, lightest, most agile, and memory-brawny machine can't keep up with him.

With time—much of it—his list of the disappeared dwindles down to the dead and those whose stubborn transparency has frustrated even the most sensitive probing and efforts of expensive private detectives. He stumbles upon a new problem: the need for fresh capital, new friends not lost, *amigos, confrères, confidantes.* So he assembles battalions of new friends, lovers, and intimates. This time, he gathers them with care, never hazarding even the single cross word, selfish gesture, forgotten birthday, anniversary, or card-appropriate holiday. His raft floats happily upon a fat sea of warm friendship. Then one day, in the midst of frenzied morning telephone calls, checking health, children, business opportunity, offering condolences for lost parents, comfort over a sister diagnosed too late with runaway uterine cancer, he senses a cross tone. A rediscovered childhood friend scoffs at his heartfelt concerns. Next, an old girlfriend is resentful, as she'd been fifteen years before, of a call he is ten minutes late in returning. First with those two, then others, they begin to drop away, like leaves from a tree, in no particular order or pattern. The sun comes out shining, the seasons change, the NASDAQ falls, rises, and falls again. His tree sheds itself, down to the last tenaciously clinging fruit. One morning finally his voice-messaging does not blink, his fax-tray lies empty, *No messages* say his various e-mail accounts. The postman delivers the week's missing-person flyer, a supermarket circular, and a sheaf of bills from the cellular company, the DSL people, the electric company, and the overnight couriers. They lie in his big green mailbox unattended for weeks.

Not to worry: He's gone off to some other place, some other thing, incognizant of this past phase.

Job

It's eleven o'clock on a Sunday night and he realizes that it's never going to get any better. He decides to jump from his window. He gets out of his bed and walks to the window and opens it. He lives on the twelfth floor, which is certainly high enough. He takes out the screen and leans it against the wall and puts one leg out the window. Far below a green awning stretches across the broad sidewalk, nearly to the street, where there's no traffic. He decides to take off his clothes to do it. If he's going to be found dead, he will be found dead naked: *Naked came I out of my mother's womb, and naked shall I return thither.* He takes off his clothes, just an old striped pajama top and boxer shorts, and folds them and places them neatly at the foot of his bed. He goes back to the window and looks down. There's no one on the street. Wait, he sees a woman walking a small dog at the opposite corner. She turns onto the avenue beyond, and the street is again quiet. He hesitates, thinking of a higher window. Some cabs pass at the end of the block. This is the twelfth floor and is high enough certainly. Be he knows of an apartment on the fifteenth, directly above his and identical in layout, that is vacant. He'd seen it on Friday morning. The building's manager had sent him up to it alone; it was unlocked. He'd decided against taking the unit because he realized then, while looking at the vacant rooms, that it was never going to get any better. He hadn't spoken yet to the rental agent, who didn't work on weekends. He goes out into hallway, glowing in its feverish state of perpetual fluorescence. The old carpet prickles his feet. Naked, he rides the elevator up three floors. The unit's door is unlocked; he enters. People have begun moving in, it seems. Whereas on Friday morning, there'd been only the smell of cheap fresh paint and a forgotten cup of coffee on the kitchen counter, now he finds half a dozen cardboard boxes sitting in the middle of the living-room floor. The refrigerator doors are closed. A mattress and box spring sit propped on end against a wall. He remembers that Dana, the rental agent, mentioned that there was another one, directly above, available as well, but that it hadn't been painted. He takes the stairs. The stairwell smells of stale air freshener. He tries the door to the unit on sixteen, but it is locked. Perhaps she'd said *two* floors; he hadn't paid much attention after deciding not to move after all. He takes the stairwell with its steel banister. He tries the door on seventeen. This door is unlocked; again he lets himself in. It is an old woman's apartment. The smell of heavy drapery and vapor rub hangs in the air. A dim table lamp burns over a desiccated tea bag that lies on a paper napkin. She is awake, he knows, in the suspended state that characterizes all but a few hours of her day. He backs out into the hallway, pulling the door shut. Nineteen. He will try one more. He does not go to twenty on the suspicion that the top floor's plan will be different. He takes the elevator, on the hope that being found naked there by someone will end this nightmare that holds him in its control. The elevator is empty; the halls are empty. He walks to the door of the same unit, the one directly above his own—1909. He tries the door. It is open. The apartment is lovely, nicely decorated in a clean, spare style. There is a sofa and an armchair and a long case full of books against one wall. He walks past the kitchen to the bedroom. There a naked woman lies upon the bed. She is tall, with long dark hair and her skin appears dark in the bluish light from the window. She is on the bed touching herself, one hand holding herself while the other works quickly. He goes to the window and opens it and takes out the screen and leans it against the wall. She says, "What are you *doing?* Come here." And he thinks of how this must be a dream. He should go to her and do what she wants him to do. That way the dream would end. But he isn't dreaming: It's no longer a dream. He puts one leg out the window. She remains lying upon the bed, but her hands are now still. They are quiet a moment. "This is crazy," she says. "How will I ever explain your jumping from my window? People will know and they will ask me and hound me over it and never let me forget. I will have to move to another city and change my name." He says, "There is no one on the street. No one in another building could tell because it is dark, unless they were looking directly at me, and even then, it would be only an approximate guess as to which window, as it is a large building, wide and tall, without any distinguishing features. There would be no way to determine from my body how far that I had fallen, unless perhaps they did some sophisticated calculations regarding my weight and impact. But it's a suicide: There would be no reason to do an autopsy or any of the figuring that would be required. They will get my name, maybe make a single call. Nobody will know why I jumped or, exactly, from where." As he says this he sees that she has started touching herself again—harder it looks to him, vigorously. And he can tell that his jumping is going to be a good thing for her. Then he begins to think about his timing. Would it be best if he went just a little before, but not too soon so she'd lose it? But what if he waits too long—so that he misses the moment, and she is finished but suddenly has this suicide to think about? He rocks on the sill, which is cool beneath him. Outside it is spring and warm. He rocks and listens to her softly moaning and the honks and sparse traffic on the avenue at the end of the block. A cab comes around the corner, slows, then speeds up again, looking for an address farther down the street. He thinks of all the people who are living in this building and the all the other people who live on the block and in those buildings that rise across the street. He thinks, what if all the people in the world I have ever known lived on this street? Surely they could be all accommodated here. Would it make any difference? It comes to him then: His existence, much as he privileged it once, is worth no more than the novelty of the moment in which he finds himself now.

Snapdragon

She padded toward Philip in thick-soled white running shoes, bent up at both ends like tiny whaleboats. The road rose at a slight incline, gradual but continuous. They—Philip pushing Audrey, the jogging woman—would meet before the old house in whose yard once stood a massive grove of bamboo. Recently, the bamboo had all been torn out. A few small switches still survived at the roadside, like decoration at the boarder of an ink drawing. The big house, previously hidden by the giant flickering green screen, looked desperate: a mottled roof, the long porch bowed, a green shutter hanging from a single hinge. It was of the shingle style—tall, airy, a ground floor crowded with pointless parlors and passages. They were all over the hills outside Baltimore: remnants of the 1890s. An old woman lived there. Or she had. Now she was dead, or filed away between the sheets in some high-density dependent care—not the comparatively luxurious retirement grounds of Broadmere, Pinkerton, or Spotteswoode at her stage. She was dead, he was sure, or so close that she would be by the time he found out exactly what had happened. The jogging woman continued steadily if slowly toward him. She bent her head, discretely wiping her nose with a curled finger, slightly breaking stride in the process. She wasn't a "runner"; from her figure alone that was plain. Not that she was ungainly—unpleasant, even. Rather, this run, at eleven A.M. on a morning two days before Christmas, was something of an exception. Perhaps it was prophylactic, against the ten days of excess and inactivity that lay ahead. She looked as if she practiced some other sport—summer tennis, say—and had taken up jogging recently, a resolution well in advance of New Year's so as not to appear faddish. Of course, she had bought the new faddish shoes, the faddish black lycra pants, a faddish red pile jacket—she was not indifferent to fashion. She was like him in that regard, he understood; were he to take up jogging, he too would first concern himself over his clothing, then second over the proper time and place. Real runners—they cared only about their shoes. The rest would be as it came: old, often washed, worn and comfortable, loose and soft. In the side yard, he noticed a child's playhouse. The clearing had revealed it. It wasn't in garish plastic colors like Audrey's, who sat silently in the stroller, but was constructed of notched logs with an asphalt shingle roof, now collapsing as if in congruity to the big house nearby. How old was it? Thirty years? No, he was thirty-five; it would have looked archaic to him as a child. Forty? Fifty? Constructed for the children, now with grown children themselves, who had slipped Mom, shrunken and half-mad (he had heard this) into dependent care. The jogging woman's slow-gaited, uphill trot brought her finally within polite hailing range. She looked first to Audrey, then to Philip. A mother herself, he could tell. She smiled nicely and said hello. He guessed her to be his age, though recently he had become unsure, in a figurative sense, about his own age. Philip returned her greeting, his voice sounding more sure than he thought that it might have. But then, why not? What reason was there for him not to be strolling his daughter through the neighborhood one morning two days before Christmas? Until recently, he had lived here as well.

The woman passed and Audrey, who had affected not to notice her at first, turned in her stroller to watch after her. Self-conscious in that regard, Philip turned and watched her go as well. She dipped her head to wipe her nose again, no doubt having been putting this off until she passed. "Bye-bye," Audrey said. The woman reached the corner and the last of the sprays of bamboo. She interested him no more going than she had when she came. Philip was doing well in that department. Audrey turned back around and settled herself in the stroller. She gave the foot rail a kick with one of her heavy red shoes. Philip had the baby because her mother was having her teeth drilled. Two days before Christmas. Why not? It just felt odd. Like the old lady's yard, denuded in December. Maybe that was the best time for it. Bamboo was nasty stuff: tough, pliant, barbed. There had been a game trail through it: raccoons; foxes, perhaps. The neighborhood dogs? He wondered what would tough through such a bramble for so little reward.

They walked to the village grocery and back again. He bought Audrey a fig bar, assuming that to be sufficiently penitential a snack. Left to his own he might have bought her a cookie studded with chocolate or a gingerbread man. It seemed to him that he ate a lot of gingerbread men as a child: four inches tall, bulbous, red-hots for features and buttons. Did red-hots even exist any longer? He would ask Tara. In any event, to prevent as much as he could any possible conflict this close to Christmas, he bought Audrey an unimpeachable fig bar. He had hated fig bars in his own childhood. They felt as if they had sand in them. The crumbly dough, the excremental color; perhaps a companion's mother served them. There was a term: companion. For a child it described a state free of volition, for an adult, one drunk with it. The clerks and stockers he knew from the grocery recognized him mostly. Only a favored cashier commented on his absence. "Work," he said. He said it in a jesting, self-deprecating way, because it was a lie. She could not have cared, really, and left the matter at that. Karen had already returned from the dentist's when they arrived back, her teeth filled, he assumed. Audrey had fallen asleep along the walk back, and Philip did not even take off his jacket. On his way out, he returned Audrey's stroller to the trunk of Karen's car, from where it had come just before she left for her appointment. From there he crossed the lawn to his car, parked in the street, and was off.

Philip went holiday shopping. He parked in the new garage that had' been built between the public library and the county court-house's extension. In 1800, Towson had lain seven hours from Baltimore by horse carriage. He had read this on a visit to the library with Audrey the week before. Geologically speaking, it was sandwiched between coastal plain below and piedmontese hills rolling northward into Pennsylvania. Culturally speaking, it was nowhere: a five-point county intersection steadily resisting renovation, improvement, or advancement. Neither derelict nor particularly thriving, it served an ugly, utilitarian purpose only. Outside the parking garage, in the awkward entry plaza of the library, Philip encountered one of his employees, a part-timer he had not seen since early fall.

"What are you doing here?" she asked, giving him an exaggerated double take when, hearing herself called by name, she recognized him. When she first came to work for him the year before, just out of college, Philip had taken an interest. Her references were all academic: glowing letters of rec from full professors at Yale. Her surname was famous in Baltimore. Philip set his secretary upon it; she was a witch after that kind of information. It came back that the young woman, named Doris, was indeed related to the famous retailing clan, as a niece. Or something. It was the gossip that attracted his secretary, and so all her information tended to have an impressionistic character to it, as all gossip does. Philip questioned why she chose to work for him. Surely money could not have been the issue. Neither was it ambition. In fact, had she been interested at all in Philip's company, she might have moved quickly up. As bright as she was—and her Yale professors were correct in that— Philip had never ascertained for certain whether she had not proceeded further because she had no interest or because it never occurred to her how easy it would be for her to succeed. Once he had thought she might become his protégé. Perhaps it had been this desire of his that she had reacted to with such aversion. Now he wished she would quit.

She explained that she had just finished a holiday shift at the big bookstore for which he headed. It was holiday-supplemental work. He might have been jealous, but for the fact that she had made their arbitrary connection so clear already. They parted with the sort of mincing, vague holiday greetings that had become commonplace, as if "Merry Christmas" were possibly some sort of slur. With good reason in this particular case, he supposed. She was Jewish. Or, at least, her family famously was. Once Philip had seen her boyfriend. He was husky—overweight, really—woolly, dressed in smelly Andean textiles. A common-cause gentile. He seemed an odd choice for an heiress, petite, redheaded, freckled. Perhaps she worked because of him.

Inside the bookstore he had three chores. First, he searched for a certain book for Audrey. It came recommended by a woman he dealt with, a sort of sentimental choice from when her children were young. When he found the book, he saw that it was too mature for his daughter, by years, really. He took it anyway. He wanted to tell this woman that he had followed her suggestion. It was a business expense and he charged it as such. Next he looked for something for Karen—but what? First he examined calendars: of Ireland, of gardens, of Maine. For what? So that she could tick off the days? Next he came to a rectory table groaning with stacks of new books. She was a reader. The few he began with seemed full of incest and drunkenness, profligate gambling and other bad habits. How happy and stable did one's life need to be to tolerate such an overabundance of borrowed misery? A book would be all wrong. He started for the staircase to the store's next level. The two of them had never been good about gifts. Always too much as to be forced, or not enough. There had never been an "exchange": hair for a fob, watch for combs. How funny: Philip at that moment just understood. Even those gifts, "perfect" as they were, would require a subsequent, postholiday tramp to the mall, an exchange, a credit slip to sit, chastening, in the jewelry box until June. He descended to the record department and turned his attention to Tara. She would call it the *music section*. "Record" to her ear sounded like "petticoat" or "castor oil" to Philip's: hopelessly dated, ancient, inutile. He had already bought Tara a present: diamond studs—large, expensive earrings that were nonetheless subtle enough not to draw too much attention to themselves. They would be their secret. The woman who had sold them to him had been quite pretty. That was a jeweler's trick, undoubtedly. Pretty, coy, flirtatious women selling women's jewelry to adulterous men; it was a ploy as old as camels probably. What would happen if you asked her out? With an undetected nod, would a bouncer materialize at your side, as he would at a naked-dancing bar? Or would she blush, and brush you off? This one Philip had seen three times, and spoken to as many times on the telephone. Probably she'd sell jewelry until someone suitable came along. Would the jeweler mind? No. He's the flower; she's the bee. Or is he the bee? Jewelers and bees? Napoleon and bees? Why? A jewel case caught his eye. A model dressed in a Santa's suit: red crush, white cuffs and collar, a stocking cap. *A Very Cocktail Christmas*. What ideal were they selling? A sort of Playboy-mansion Christmas, he supposed. Shapely women dancing about in short fur capes, naked underneath. Mixed drinks. Slim guys wearing sharkskin suits. Pocket squares and quilted smoking jackets. For women of Karen's—and his—age, the image represented the registered trademark of sexism, oppression, misogyny. Petticoats, castor oil. For women Tara's age, ten years younger, somehow it all seemed fun—assertive, even, of one's identity and power. Maybe Tara's mother had been a Bunny. Tara came from St. Paul. A Playboy Club must have rotated about the top of some downtown Minneapolis Radisson in the late sixties: fishnet stockings, long blonde hair, sleeveless Bunny suits, bow ties, big black organza bows at back. How long since there had been Bunnies? He might be right; he'd seen a photo of Tara's mother as a young woman: a fashion photograph, in fact. Perhaps she sold jewelry by day. Philip would have to ask Tara that. Not the jewelry, but if her mother had ever been a Bunny. She would laugh. In reality, he knew little of her family. Philip wandered into the next aisle of the music section and selected another disk—not the one with the suggestive art, but a collection along similar lines. This isn't a fantasy, he thought with a fulsome twinge not unlike the one he had felt upon the stairs. This is happening. He took the album and the book for Audrey and joined the cue that snaked all the way to Latin America.

He waited his turn in the holiday chain gang. Ahead of him stood a mismatched couple: older, miserable, glum. The man held two mingy albums—gifts for a stepchild. Already they represented a resented outlay of time and money. Behind him a young woman, college-aged, stood seriously gripping some other disk as if it were the first thing she had ever bought. Her prettiness, her potential, all lay in her youth. She was like a ghost, a shade of all college-aged women that ever were, all college-aged girls to come. Across the long narrow department—the basement of the building—whose dark green carpet pulled the low ceilings even lower, Philip recognized another face. She stood at the service desk, impassively awaiting the research of a goateed and denim-shirted clerk. Philip had dated her twice, eight years before. Since then and still, he saw her twice annually, always coincidentally. There were women living in Baltimore with whom he had been to Europe, women whom he'd nearly married, women in Baltimore with whom he had complex and troubling histories. He would not mind seeing most of them again, if only for the involuntary, visceral thrill it would bring. He never did. But he saw this woman twice a year, invariably. Each time, she looked directly at him, and then away. In contempt? Superciliousness? She had come by it honestly, certainly. As usual, she spotted him before he saw her. Their shared glance contained its usual, brief burst of mutual discomfort. It was as if her annoyance at him, and his annoyance at being reminded of it, was set to last, in this stable condition, a lifetime. What could she be ordering? Classical? Foreign language? Lesbian? The line crept ahead over the carpet. Christmas music, contemporary, over the hidden speakers. Of the three cashiers, one was black, one olive-skinned, and one redheaded, with thick beautiful hair. Philip had read recently that redheads were the most sought-after of women due to their relative scarcity. Redheaded woman had never interested him before that. Now he took notice. The line spurted forward again. Could it be that, rather than being the result of maternal love and the first skinned-knee and sand-flecked infatuations, a man's preferences were really only market driven? Were they trendy and variable, like an emergent interest in Thai cookery or a newfound sporting interest in cycling? Philip set about calculating his odds of being rung up by the redhead. This was why he had labored at calculus. The black woman appeared easily distracted. The dark-haired (Lebanese? Iranian?), no doubt a fill-in like Doris, fumbled with the antitheft device. Barring a sudden newfound interest by the one woman in her task, or an epiphanic insight into the demagnetizer by the other, the redheaded cashier would be his. Then she left. In her relief arrived a squat, poorly dressed woman, also redheaded, oddly enough. She called to Philip. It wasn't diamond earrings he was purchasing, after all. As he left the department, sack in hand, he passed along the line, which now stretched back to discount country. The woman he dated twice waited toward its end. Seeing Philip seeing her, she turned to reach for something from easy listening. Outside, the forty minutes spent shopping had done nothing to alter the flat cast of still gray stamping the sky.

Along his way back downtown, he passed a car driven by a woman wearing a Santa's stocking cap. She caught his eye; they smiled: a brief exchange at eighteen miles per hour, rounding the corner of Old Court and Falls Roads. At a few minutes past six, he waited at the Baltimore harbor, beneath the estuarine hulk of the World Trade Center. Lights twinkled about the edge of the black basin, many miles from any sea. As such, it was startling, like coming upon a building standing within a building, or seeing the profile of a large ship traveling along a river you have not yet reached. The peaked skylights of the aquarium looked a dingy gray in the winter dark. A giant neon sign, shaped like a guitar, hung along a dark stack of the disused power station, so crass as to be nearly unremarkable. Lights shone farther out, strung along the tree of a ship in demurrage at the sugar plant. Otherwise, the old harbor had been cleared of maritime function, and the vast spaces between what remained, once crowded with piers and ships and stores, now blew with a haunting wind.

Tara pulled open the car door and that same wind, damp and metallic, followed her. She worked there, in the World Trade Center. Philip and his partner had used an architect to design their expansion: new offices and an enlarged shop. Tara was a marketer for the architect they hired. She'd bring by blueprints, swatches, cabinetry veneers. Philip thought he'd met her the first time she came; it was the second. She caught him entirely by surprise. And his surprise had been returned by her—almost, he thought, involuntarily. Their romance, then, proceeded in a quick and orderly way: So much had been accomplished in the first moment of their meeting. In reality, the architects for whom she worked hadn't done a very good job. The result turned out to be distinctly middle-score, without even the small comfort of the current design clichés. They certainly weren't "difficult." In fact, they weren't good enough, even, to be derivative. As a result, the renovation had left him with dreary offices and an inefficient floor. His partner barely noticed, however, and Philip had met Tara. He could take solace in that at least. In the end, she was like the woman who sold jewelry. Already, she was looking for another job. "Marketers" always were.

Quickly the car filled with her scent: the leather of her jacket and the tang of her lip gloss, the light perfume she wore and the vague hint of the occasional cigarettes sneaked on the pier with her young co-workers. Philip's professional disappointment with her employers did not mean to suggest that he wasn't wholly in love. As they drove around the arc of the harbor and back toward Mount

Vernon—midtown—he felt again the spontaneous exhilaration that came always when they were together. How to explain it? The contracting of the heart, the tingling, the feeling of fullness—he felt them all when they were together, especially at first. Tara indulged him in this; she was quite at ease in the role of the prettiest. She was twenty-five.

They dined out, as they did nearly every night they were together. This evening they went to a new Italian restaurant they liked behind the cathedral. It was crowded in its early resplendence. They ate there enough to be known, and the place had a safe, settled feeling for him. Still, Philip could look sufficiently in upon his situation to see the folly. He had become a regular at the city's most expensive restaurant. From dinner they walked to a party in the neighborhood. It was held in one of the Mount Vernon Square townhouses proper, which belonged to the principal of an ad shop with which Tara did business. She had been invited as a client, Philip supposed, though the party—by the look of things, started after work—felt so casual, even edgy, that he assumed her to have a more intimate relation with the shop than a merely professional one. There was a little bit of the gay thing going on: costuming and campy music, a smell of esters, and men all scrummed up in one corner. That was unavoidable in this neighborhood. When the shop's director appeared, from a bedroom, he gave Philip a wary look, as if desperate to be assured that he was not some paying client who stumbled in by accident. The sight of Tara behind him seemed to calm him. Philip recognized something of himself in the man: Someone who had become moderately successful at what was essentially a frivolous trade; or, rather, a business that traded in frivolity. Introduced, they exchanged sympathetic nods. But for one or two other exceptions, Philip and this man were the oldest people there.

In the large, refurbished kitchen, three men stood around a table on which sat a bowl, a bottle of brandy, and a red box of raisins. They all looked to be Tara's age; one wore a goatee, one short hair and sideburns, and the other, who was black, a small diamond stud in one ear. He and the goateed guy wore khaki trousers; the other wore jeans. All three wore thick leather belts with shiny chromed buckles. Their shoes had thick, cluttered rubber soles, as if their work might require scrambling. The one with the goatee poured brandy into the bowl, then sprinkled the brandy liberally with raisins. Philip watched them from an unnoticed distance. Tara had disappeared into the crowd. He wondered about their clothing. They were all dressed neatly, fussily even, and carefully groomed. It was a catalogue look, he realized, a sort of uniform they wore. The one with the goatee took a lighter from his trousers' pocket and put it to the brandy. The bowl flared yellow, causing him to jump back, then fell to a blue, auroral glow. The three seemed to discuss what came next. The one with the goatee, the instigator, no doubt, reached into the flame to snatch at a raisin. The other two laughed. The one with sideburns tried after him, failing as well. The black guy stood back at a distance. It was snapdragon they were playing, Philip realized with a start, the Twelfth Night game that his English grandmother had taught him as a child. How could these young men know?

> Snapdragon, snapdragon, now we all come,
> Put in a finger and pull out a plum—

and its admonitory warning:

> Only take care that you don't burn your thumb.

The bowl cracked loudly. Brandy began to seep out onto the tabletop. The look of initial shock on their faces turned to guilty mirth. They poured the brandy from the bowl into the sink; one of them wiped the table with a napkin. They left the kitchen in single file and dispersed out into the party. Tara appeared at his side. She had found a red stocking cap with white fringe, which she wore.

Between the dinner and the party, Tara had managed to drink a lot, which in his experience Philip found unusual. They left and walked back across the square, now cold and gritty-feeling, to the car, and drove to Philip's. He had taken an apartment in the Mies-designed building on North Charles. In the spartan, see-through lobby, Tara's green eyes (more green still for the red stocking cap she still wore at a jaunty low angle) twinkled at Lenny or Lou, the night guy. Lenny (he was certain it was Lenny) responded with an enthusiastic and serious charm. Beautiful, Tara expected attention from men; a little drunk, she seemed to be enjoying it. How different it all felt. How rare and manufactured. They entered the elevator, leaving Lenny just outside the closed doors below, hanging on Tara's last long glance. She kissed Philip. In his apartment he opened a bottle of champagne. He gave her the Christmas album, which she put on the player, its volume up much too loud. He turned off the lights. From the bedroom's full windows, the city lay below, twinkling all the way to the harbor. She undressed but for the red stocking cap. When he was her age, someone like Tara would have intimidated him. This was what they meant, he thought as they fell to the bed. This was a cocktail Christmas. Here was the fantasy. The city lights looked warm from bed: an illusion. Finally, she fell away to sleep.

The next day was hardly any less pleasant. Tara awoke feeling rocky but dragged herself to a half-day's work. Philip talked on the telephone most of the morning. He sat beside the window, look-ing out over the whiskey-brown manger of the city. By noon, the sun had begun to shine, spottily, showing the landscape below. In the light, the city lacked the melancholy it had projected from be-neath the clouds. Now it asserted only solstitial despair. Philip went shopping. Again he went north, to Towson. The mall. Regardless of the crowds and the anxious parking, he found himself enjoying it. He had never been Christmas shopping before—or at least not since he was a child. And while he had assumed Christmas Eve shopping to be an act of desperation, instead he found around him a self-confident calm: as if, when else would one do it? At the cook-ery store he bought a saucier and German cutlery, French porce-lain and big, glorious wooden spoons. He even let the shop person wrap them: five big green boxes' worth. Likewise, he enjoyed the chaos of the Roland Park grocery. It was a gourmet grocery: in industry terms, "specialty and gourmet." It was specialty and gourmet as best as he could tell because they sold olives, some goat cheeses, and assorted mustards. Nevertheless, it was a good grocer's and he had gotten to know the clerks and a meatman. He bought caviar and sea bass and filets. He bought two good bottles of wine and more champagne. Back outside the grocery, the hard pewter light had toned to gold, and the lawns and the low houses of his neighborhood had about them a sort of gloriole. He caught the scent of firewood in the air. From his apartment's windows, he saw a fat band of mulberry-colored sky upon the horizon.

Christmas Eve, then, had begun. He did not labor much over dinner; he wasn't a cook. He did manage to open all his boxes and use all the tools he had bought. After their meal, they exchanged gifts. Tara began with a barrage of small things—a few of which were somewhat curious, as if her carefully affected youth and hipness had hit a sort of conceptual block when shopping for an older lover's Christmas gifts. Still, her production set the stage nicely for what was to follow. He gave her his single small gift, carefully wrapped by the pretty woman at the jewelers. (She had done quite a nice job in her wrapping; unexpected with her nails and her hair and her carefully applied makeup, all of which suggested more experience in opening gifts than wrapping them.) Tara prolonged the moment until it brought tears to his eyes. She greeted the studs with an unmistakable appreciation. They fulfilled something elemental. Not something base, necessarily: simply basic. No one had given her diamonds before, or at least diamonds approaching that magnitude. She had planned, if not exactly counted, on it, and here that wish had been fulfilled. There followed another romantic parley: a fantastical indulgence, really. He visited again in his mind the image on the album jacket. A blonde woman wearing a short red velour dress edged in white fur, a stocking cap perched jauntily on her head. Green eyes twinkling. Unreal. A fantasy, and yet, here it had happened to him, was happening to him, as the same music played over and over on the stereo in the other room.

The next morning Tara woke in an uneasy mood: no tree, perhaps, no more presents (he scolded himself for not considering this). It was another piebald day. She had forgone returning to St. Paul for the first time ever. Initially, the idea had been hers; he assumed that in the end she would go. She delighted in the illusion of independence and self-reliance. He had asked her not to say much yet about them to her parents—with her remaining for the holidays in Baltimore, he assumed that she had not honored that wish. Now he could tell she was rethinking. She suddenly missed the Swedish pancakes, the snow on the ground, the piles of gilded wrapping paper. She longed for the hurried morning festivities to be followed by the big family dinner: turkey or sauerbeef. When, shortly before eleven, he prepared to leave, she affected to be furious. By virtue of her application, her manufactured indignation quickly converted itself into real fury. Had he told her? To be honest, he had not. He had hoped that, blonde, attractive, unattached, in her first real job, and dating a man older by ten years, she might recognize on her own that some portion of Christmas Day, at least, would be spent with his family. "What am I to do?" she asked. "Sit at home by myself?" She stormed out; he caught her at the elevator. Not so subtly, he admired her earrings. She cried now. He promised they would spend the afternoon together. They'd talk just after lunch.

The drive to Ruxton had a funerary feel to it. The lawns looked a thin green. Again the clouds had broken, leaving a bright, characterless day. Audrey met him at the door. He was unsure what she understood. She knew now that he only "visited"; otherwise she seemed to him unaffected by the current state of affairs. Conversely, her looks and the thoughts they appeared to convey suggested that she knew everything and was already scheming far ahead. Karen's mother, Regina, had arrived already and installed herself on the

couch closest to the fire. She regarded him silently, heavy with reproach and blame. Another woman, a divorced neighbor in her
fifties, emerged from the kitchen ahead of Karen, who carried a tray
of china tea cups. Philip passed them and went through the door
into the kitchen—for no reason other than to escape Regina's con-
demnatory stare. She was a profoundly ignorant woman whose con-
temning and pompous religiosity had not kept her from raising a
daughter who was an adulteress. The tray on the stool at her
mother's feet, Karen returned alone to the kitchen. Why was he to
blame? He wasn't the one who had slept with the vice president of
a building supply company going public. It wasn't Philip who'd gone
to Nevis with him, on a lumber junket. She'd left *him*. And because
the guy had a wife and two children of his own, and because it became too complicated for him, and he withdrew, by stages, from the
affair—somehow, by virtue of that reprehensible behavior, on both
parties' part, it was *Philip* who was dealt reproach because he would
not return home? These same thoughts, which had crossed his
mind so many times each day that they had worn a trail—they
rushed past him in fury, as if new, again. Karen began to speak.

"Merry Christmas," he said. He passed her to re-enter the living room and its silent abuse.

The gift exchange proceeded slowly, without much happiness.
Most of the gifts were for Audrey, anyway. Philip had brought nothing for either Karen or her mother. He hadn't known that Holly
was coming. Karen gave him a book—something about happy living or a life well lived. Regina gave him an accusatory bar of scented
soap. He could not wait to throw both of them into an anonymous
dumpster on the way home. Noon came and went, then one. He
had understood that they were to have lunch together. The meal,
whatever it was to be, seemed to be slow in coming together. There
was no chance to make a telephone call—who would he say he was
calling? Karen knew nothing of Tara; he had been careful to keep
that from her. And had he called, what would he tell Tara? He went
to the kitchen to make himself a drink. He supposed that he could.

The vodka remained where he had left it, and the vermouth. Karen followed him. There was something in the oven after all: a capon. Karen opened the oven door to check on it.

"Are you staying tonight?" she asked without any other introduction. In the five months that he had been gone, he had spent the night twice. Both times he neither particularly regretted nor felt strongly compelled to repeat the experience soon thereafter. After both times he assumed it would happen again. They were not formally separated. However, the last time had been in October, when he had only just begun seeing Tara. He did not respond at first. The situation had changed, and he felt his wife to have some advantage over him. Karen remained squatted before the open oven. Its furnace air had begun to moisten the baby's down that lay forever undisturbed just below her hairline. She was still a pretty woman. She had proved that. "I can't tonight," he said. His voice had little confidence to it, no timbre whatsoever. He took a guilty drink. Karen's eyes filled with tears. "Are you going to see . . . her?" Her?

"Oh, don't even . . . " Karen waved a red-mitted hand. She tugged at the oven rack. "I know about her, your girlfriend." She poked at the capon roasting in the enameled pan, not checking the thermometer, just following the empty gestures of the profoundly depressed. She returned the rack and closed the oven door. Rather than rising, she remained upon her knees. She pressed her forehead against the oven door's black handle. He took another drink. Expensive oven. "When are you going to stop?" She was crying. She whispered through her tears. "Stop with the punishment?" He put his drink down on the countertop. Short of breath, he knew that he would need to hold her. Karen stood and stepped into his embrace. She was so heavy compared to the lightness of Tara in his arms. He smelled the roasting carrots and onions about her, and felt the crisp linen of her holiday apron and the pressed cotton blouse she wore and the smell of her soaps and perfume. Karen had not changed much from the time that Philip first met her. She dressed the same, wore the same scents. She had come to him fully formed. They had grown so little together that the possibility of adultery, when it arose, required no thought. She never considered how it might affect her husband. He knew that. She had said as much. And as much as he wanted to believe otherwise—because he was a romantic and a sentimentalist at base—he knew that, though she desired him to return, she could never absolutely rule out, were she to be honest, leaving him again.

Philip did not arrive back at the Mies building until four. He reached Tara after two tries. She agreed to come over only because, he knew, she could not face the thought of spending her evening alone. She would make him wait a long time. He called his parents in Oregon. Against his better judgment, he confided to his mother his exchange with Karen. She too asked him when he would return. It was as if, by some protracted civil court battle, the original facts of the case had been rendered unrecognizable by motion and countersuit. Now all that remained was a point of law: Philip as a husband and father abroad. Once he had hung up with Oregon, the telephone rang. He considered not taking it, but for that it might have been Tara. Instead, it was an old roommate from college calling. He lived now in Houston, married to a woman he'd met in business school. They had two children and what seemed, from photos, a large house. He worked for an oil company, traveled, owned a sailboat, still spoke decent French. They had married five years before Philip and Karen had, and had two children very quickly. "They're planning a big family," Karen always said, though Philip never knew that from his friend Robert. After they had talked around the usual—the breakup was still new to him—Robert said: "So, do you know any young pregnant women in Baltimore who don't want to keep the child?" Philip, who had opened a bottle of wine when his mother came on the phone and had now drunk more of it than he'd intended to, felt a paranoid rush: Had he mentioned Tara to him before? If Karen knew, then did everyone? And what sort of bizarre comment was that? "You think I'm kidding," Rob went on. "Really, we're looking to adopt." Why, Philip asked, with the two kids they already had—a lovely family, very happy. Why? Robert explained that they'd always wanted a bigger family and had tried all the tricks, the treatments. Seven years—they had gone the whole route. "Don't worry, Phil," he said in the joking Texas way he had increasingly assimilated over the past seven years. "There're still plenty of nice little white girls out there that need a home."

Philip left the kitchen, went to the window. In the roadbed below, he spotted Tara's car, a small yellow coupe pulling onto Charles Street. He could hear in their last conversation that she had crested some sort of hill with him. In three months—because three months is a terrifically long time were you're twenty-five—he would be history. Thick clouds stacked along a darkened horizon. He thought he heard the treadle of little feet clopping across the loose parquets, the clatter of a dragged toy. His eyes began to water and his sinuses started to collapse. He would not allow himself the ultimate masculine indulgence of crying. He didn't deserve it. Still, he believed himself to be the one originally wronged. That, he knew, had been forgotten otherwise. *Snapdragon, snapdragon, now we all come.* "I've left my daughter," he said aloud to the thick black pane of insulated glass. "What kind of man leaves his child?"

Counterfactuals

Charlotte fires the cleaning people, whom she feels have been an extravagance. For a while, Curtis tries cleaning the house himself. He dry mops the wood floors, then cleans spots of grit or grime using a squirt bottle containing a homemade mixture of lemon and ammonia and a soft towel. He puts on yellow latex gloves and cleans the bathrooms, scrubbing and wiping down the commode and the basins and spritzing the mirrors with the same lemon and ammonia solution he uses on the floor. The next weekend there are various chores to do that prevent him from cleaning, and he has to work all the weekend after that. The following Saturday morning, he glances at the paper, drinks a cup of coffee, then goes to the utility closet for the blue plastic bucket and the yellow gloves and the squirt bottle of lemon and ammonia. He works his way to the upstairs bathroom, where he cleans the shower stall. He stretches to swab down a distant corner of the stall floor, where the caulk is turning a little dusky with mildew along the black base tiles. His nose tingles with the ammonia fumes and trickles of sweat begin to run from his temples, threatening to stream into his eyes. He sits back on his heels in a catcher's stance, as if the shower stall might deliver him a sudden knuckleball or slider. He sets down the sponge and the pump bottle of ammonia and lemon and strips off his yellow gloves. Charlotte is playing interleague tennis. He decides to leave her.

It is his birthday, and he's sitting in the evening twilight, alone, waiting for Charlotte to return from a trip to Crisfield, where she went to buy a chest of drawers. He decides to leave her.

He is sitting at his desk in his office after a long, bitter, and corrosive phone call from Charlotte. She has told him not to bother coming home. He decides to leave her.

He is in the main lobby of the Inn at Williamsburg, guests of Charlotte's parents for the January Antiques Forum. He is waiting for Charlotte to come down from the room to go to dinner. Tall men in blazers and slacks drink old-fashioneds. Middle-aged women with set hair in honey blonde chirp at the window to the lobby shops. He decides to leave her.

Whenever it is, he decides. He decides to leave Charlotte and he goes.

He begins seeing a trim, self-confident blonde woman who does public relations for the architectural firm designing a new building at work. They move in together and then buy a townhouse in Washington. They marry and move to Miami Beach, where she finds new work, and they live in a tall apartment tower overlooking the water. Four nights a week they eat out at dark, fascinating restaurants. At their favorite of them they have their own booth. They make many friends: Cubans, Anglos, blacks, and Israeli transplants. After her mother dies, they begin spending parts of their summers at a lake in Michigan where her family has a cabin. After ten years in Miami, they buy a house on the Gulf Coast—Naples— and begin spending all of their summers at the lake. Her youngest brother begins going through his own messy divorce—rehab, bankruptcy, and restraining orders. They adopt the brother's youngest daughter, her niece, and she lives with them in Naples until she graduates from high school.

He begins seeing a French woman just two years his junior who, married disastrously at twenty, has been living in the United States ever since, working for the World Bank in Washington as an analyst. They fall in love. When both their divorces come through, she decides to change jobs, and they move to New York. She works at a merchant bank with French connections. It's an extremely good and lucrative job, the likes of which she might have had years before but for being tied down by her jealous husband, a pediatrician. Money is suddenly plentiful, and Curtis takes a job writing for a neighborhood newspaper. This leads to working in development for the New York City Public Library, when his wife's partner becomes a trustee. They live in a fantastic apartment and, between his job and hers, entertain there often. They begin traveling to France, which her first husband never allowed. Her family, grateful after such a long separation, welcomes them warmly. Ten years seem to fly by. She retires from the bank and they travel the country—to Las Vegas, Detroit, Houston—places that enchant her precisely for their American absurdity. After a few years of this, a cousin who is expanding a cognac firm asks them to represent it in the United States. For the next several years, this becomes their shared hobby, casually attending food fairs and wine events. The cognac becomes quite popular, and the firm is bought by a European luxury goods conglomerate.

He leaves his wife, finds an apartment near the Inner Harbor. He sees his daughter, a sophomore at the Bryn Mawr School, twice a week for dinner and on alternate weekends. On her vacations he takes her skiing or sailing. He dates wildly at first, sometimes going out five nights a week. There are a few half-hearted relationships, then an ill-advised commitment that ends worse than his marriage did. He remains alone, not even dating, for nearly two years. Twice he moves in that time, until he finds an apartment he's comfortable in. That fall he begins seeing a print-making instructor at the Maryland Institute College of Art, a woman who is married to a sculptor living and teaching in Kansas City. In the end, though she loves Curtis, she cannot break up her own marriage; her life is too comfortable as it is.

He meets a woman with whom he falls very quickly in love. They date for a year, quarrel violently, and break up. He finds himself heartbroken over the separation. She takes him back, with all sorts of conditions and caveats. There is a constant threat of termination hanging over his head. However, they live in contented happiness, mostly, because he is in love with her in a manner he had never considered possible. As they age, and certain resentments inevitably solidify, he still loves her without measure. They lead a migratory life, ending up in a modest house in Pasadena, California, where she works as an editor at a trade newspaper in Glendale. In the evenings, when the sun sets, his street runs with golden light, and the smell of the fragrant shrubbery fills his nose as strongly as the first day he arrived. He stands at the gate to their small California garden, waiting for her to arrive home.

Curtis remains in his crouch, on his heels. Ammonia and lemon fills his nostrils. The hastening dust gathers around the Adirondack chair in which he sits, mosquitoes nibbling at his ankles. He stares through the window panes at the naked barrenness of the Williamsburg golf course green, its graveled cart paths daubed with snow. What if? he asks himself.

On the Night before Her Birthday

On the night before her birthday, after Sigrid's husband had excused himself from the dinner table to return telephone calls, she asked her daughter, "Am I getting a new car for my birthday?" They were eating in the dining room, because this was the first night Tony had been home for nearly a week; Sigrid cooked lemon chicken and lit candles. In a sense, the formality was premature; presumably the next evening's dinner, of which her husband had taken control, would be festive. This was in anticipation to a degree. Temperamental, she preferred gentle transitions to abrupt changes and positively hated surprises, which is why the car had become something of a critical issue. If she was getting the car—and she had to begun to strongly suspect that she was—she would be wonderfully happy. She really wanted the car. If she didn't get the car, a dark blue German station wagon, then she would spend the next few weeks, a month perhaps, doing whatever was needed to force Tony to buy her the car because she had decided she really wanted it. However, if for some reason she believed that she *was* going to get the car, but didn't, and this happened on the day of her birthday, then there would be a problem—a very serious problem.

So she asked her daughter if she was getting a car. Her daughter, who was ten, smiled her huge-toothed smile but remained silent. "I just don't want to get my hopes up if I'm not," Sigrid said. Her daughter smiled wider and shrugged. She was getting a car.

The next morning, she woke happy and expectant and put on her blue satin robe with the white piping and descended the back stairs to the kitchen. Tony, dressed for work, and Caroline for school, sat side by side at the solarium table, half a dozen brightly wrapped packages before them. A huge slice of glorious morning light made the presents glitter.

"Well," Sigrid said happily. "What have we here?"

Tony beamed the way he did when particularly proud, a smile, Sigrid knew from experience, that could melt easily to tears. Caroline had the same electric, almost foolish look upon her face: Tony's wide, goofy grin, but with the Stennerson family's big teeth.

"*Mom*," Caroline said, drawing out the name and rattling the first of the presents, as if she were attracting a dog.

"First things first," said Sigrid, now fully intent upon extracting from the day, which she knew now would fulfill her dreams, its maximum pleasure. Her birthday: the day of her birth. "Let me get my coffee." Tony had made coffee, which sat in its hourglass carafe on the range's simmer-plate. He'd squeezed a glass of orange juice for her as well. She opened the cabinet and reached to the back for a ceramic mug, hand painted in Yorkshire, a little treasure that she used only on special occasions. She poured the coffee, added a fillip of milk, and picked up her glass of fresh juice. The tiled counters glistened, the butcher block smelled of lemon, and the porcelain vegetable sink with its heavy brass fixtures shone with preternatural brightness in the clear light of the spring morning. Sigrid settled herself at the table, at her usual spot in the full light. "Now," she said, while reaching for a slice of fragrant cantaloupe. "Where to begin?"

Caroline pushed the package in her direction. Slowly, drawing out the sensuous pleasure of the first gift, Sigrid opened it. It con-

tained a device for the grilling of fish. Lately, Sigrid had been in-
sisting that the family eat more fish. It was healthful. Caroline
needed to develop the taste. Tony could use a break from his steak,
and little else, that he ate every night. He objected to fish on the
grounds that the odor of cooking made its way to the living room—
upstairs, even. He didn't like foreign smells in the house, and,
frankly, didn't like fish, even if he did agree with his wife's argu-
ments regarding its nutritional aspects and more friendly impact on
the environment. Tony was an environmentalist, if a banker. "Come
spring, you can cook fish outside on the grill," she remembered him
saying.

Next came something heavy and ovular: Indeed, it was an oval
platter, gaily painted in Italy, for serving fish. At this point Sigrid
entertained her first doubt—it was an expensive piece of crockery
and she saw a theme developing. Could Tony's wide smile when she
first came down the stairs have been over his remembering his
promise about *fish?*

The next package she opened contained a bundle of three
French hand towels, woven throughout with tiny fish. Sigrid felt
herself begin to panic. Caroline slid the next present her way,
which, hands beginning to shake, Sigrid opened. It was a padded
barbecue mitt in the shape of a marlin. The next gift from the last
was obviously a book; Sigrid barely had the courage to open it. Her
coffee sat going cold; she had not touched her juice but for the first
delighted exploratory sip. It was almost as if a cloud were passing
overhead. She ran her fingers beneath the folds of the clerk-
wrapped paper, bent back the clinging tape, and turned the book
over: *Fish on the Grill.*

The last unopened gift on the table was an envelope. She knew
before opening it what it would be. That is, she knew exactly what
it *wouldn't* be. It wouldn't hold the title to a gleaming blue German
station wagon, or its registration; it wouldn't hold a photograph of
that blue car she wanted and airline tickets to retrieve it in Munich.

It wouldn't hold a simple business card of the man at the automotive dealer's to contact regarding choices of interior and color. It would not contain some space-age key. No. It would include a handwritten note from Tony, explaining why there would be no car.

Sigrid had wanted a new car for some time; she had never liked hers from the beginning. It had been her mother-in-law's, a luxury Japanese car, chosen to suit the taste of a woman whose living room was carpeted in gold plush. Part of the problem with the car—beyond its champagne color, gold trim, sick-beige interior, and crummy cassette deck—was that, to Sigrid's mind at least, she could never get it clean. To begin, the car's interior had about it always the hint of cigarette smoke, though Tony's mother had died of lung cancer just three months after purchasing it. In the years—eight—since, its paint had faded; city driving, with its dog's life of pricks and pocks, had made it coarse. Its hood in the sunlight made her think of her own complexion—in the bright lights of her mirrored bath— and made her feel old and coarse herself. It made her think about how much she wanted from life but had never gotten.

On the last day of March, after a winter that had been black with rain and sorrow, she pulled into the dealership in Towson; the exact model she wanted was on the showroom floor. As a consequence of Tony's outrageous hours, not to mention his strict opinions on labor division, Sigrid spent hours stacked upon hours driving around north Baltimore. She trekked from Homeland to Roland Park Country School and, every third weekday, from RPCS to the scattered homes of the girls in Caroline's car pool. In summer there were camps. In the winter they went to a riding stable out in the county. There were piano lessons in Timonium, the pediatrician at Greenspring Station, twice-weekly visits to the allergist in Hunt Valley. Sigrid spent her waking life in her car. God forbid Tony ever pick up from gymnastics. She wanted a new car.

Quickly, an attractive guy in a bad sports coat approached her.

He was in his early thirties, she guessed. They went to his cubicle and discussed options with two glossy brochures and a chain of leather swatches spread over her lap. He picked up the telephone and read out an alphanumeric code to someone in the lot. "I may have something here," he said, hanging up. "It doesn't have the rims you were looking at, but it does have a better sound system. It has the undercoating you said you didn't want, but I could throw that in. Otherwise it's the right color and interior."

When the car came around, driven by a little man in a striped shirt, Sigrid felt the way she had when she got her first puppy. The car was so new that protective masking covered the roof and the rocker panels. Every seat but the driver's was still covered in plastic. Incredibly, the odometer had only 2.2 miles on it. This car would never smell of cigarettes; it would never be anything but wholly and completely hers.

"Take it," said the dealer, whose name, comically, was Chip. He waved vaguely up York Road. "If you turn right on Paper Mill, the road goes right around Loch Raven reservoir. It's kind of neat."

"You don't need to . . . ?" she asked.

"No, no," he said, waving again. "Take it home with you if you want. Make sure you like it."

She drove cautiously at first, fiddling with the mirrors, adjusting the seat, poking guiltily at the radio. The multiplicity of new buttons and toggles made her fingers tingle. The dash glowed such a seductive color of green that she could have pulled onto the shoulder and stared contentedly at it alone. Beneath low clouds, the road was dark from the drizzle that had fallen all morning. She felt elation so complete that she could only imagine that she was in some other country, some other skin, a movie.

By the time Sigrid turned back, nearly an hour later, into the dealership, she had traveled thirty-five miles (her miles!) through a full cycle of emotions. First she had decided it couldn't happen; it was too insane. She never pictured herself as the sort of person who walked onto a car lot and bought the first car she drove. There had to be haggle and back and forth, gamesmanship, not to mention the diligent trudge to every place selling similar wares in three states. Tony couldn't buy toothpaste (were he ever to grocery shop) without first assuring himself that he had somehow received a deal, or a quid pro quo in the form of a fishing trip to Montana or an invitation to ski in Idaho. But was that the way *she* really was? For so long she had entertained no goal other than to be Mrs. Anthony Baugher; perhaps she'd succeeded so completely that she'd forgotten or—worse still—never become herself.

She decided that the car—this car—would be hers; she would drive it home. It was a good car, a respectable car, if expensive. They could afford it. Despite Tony's monthly cries of poverty, their house was worth over a million. Tony had his own company (a local distribution fleet) and was on the board of directors at his family's bank. The Baughers as a family were loaded, had always been loaded, and would remain loaded, even with the purchase of one dark blue German luxury station wagon. It was exactly the car she wanted, in every aspect; the superior radio over the rims, even, she found to be an excellent trade.

"Listen," Chip said. "It's the last day of the month. Is there a chance you might be interested in driving this car home today?"

Sigrid looked at the small triangle of a calendar on the dealer's desk. Indeed it was March thirty-first. She called Tony's office from the cubical feeling confident. Chip had politely excused himself to "check on something." When she reached her husband she heard the squeak of his office chair as he sat upright. The discussion was swift and certain. She barely had the chance to tell him where she was calling from.

"We are *not* buying a car today," he shouted at her and hung up.

Sigrid paused before reading the card. Her hands were shaking visibly now. Without looking up, she could see Tony's wide grin and her daughter's expectant gaze. She opened it.

COMPLETE DETAILING!
A $79.99 Gift Certificate
for a complete detailing at
WASH WORLD!

Beneath, Tony had written:

Sweetie,

This isn't the year for a new car. Maybe next birthday, we'll see. With
a good clean all over, you'll feel better about the car you have now,
and it will be okay for a while.

Love, Tony

The telephone rang, and with her already jangled nerves, it
made her jump, shocking the tears back into her. Caroline got up
from the table and answered.

"Mom, it's Cissy Lord. She can't drive car pool this morning,
can you?"

Instinctively, Sigrid looked at the clock above the table. She and
Cissy Lord and Ellen May alternated car pool for their daughters,
who were within a grade of each other at RPCS.

"Tony, can you take them?" she asked, setting aside the card.

"Got a meeting downtown, babe," he said, with less venom than
usual when asked to perform a domestic task. Perhaps he was still
satisfied with himself over the themed gifts. "Cannot do it."

Sigrid pushed herself up from the table. "Tell Cissy I'm fine,
love," she said. "I'll drive." Immediate activity would keep her from
saying something she might later regret. It would allow her to get
on with her day, another day, like any other of her hopeless and un-
livable days. As she struggled up the back stairs she forced herself
to recall her strategy: No car just meant getting the car later, another project, more drives, more cloudy afternoon transports. The
only concern had been to protect her feelings. It wasn't about the
car. But she'd failed to protect herself; again she'd allowed herself
to be sucked into unrealistic expectations—expectations of satis-

faction, of contentedness. It would never come; there was none of that to be found in her life.

By the time she reached her mirrored bathroom, her eyes were again fat with tears. She got the spigot rushing with cold water before she began to sob. Her cheeks burned, her chest heaved, and no amount of the cold water that she cupped, handful after handful over her face, could put out the fire—not fire but radiation, the burning of the decaying poison in her body. She stripped off her blue robe and let it fall. With one hand still splashing her face, she climbed from her green silk pajamas until she was standing naked in the large room, surrounded entirely by mirrors. Sigrid had remained slim; she'd always been slim. And if not nineteen anymore, she was still comely, she knew. She knew. Bracing her hands on the lip of the basin, she looked at herself in the mirror, her eyes shot with blood, her nose running, her lips turning down and wobbling uncontrollably. The room began to spin. She stumbled back and sat upon the toilet lid. She sensed herself tumbling into a funnel or a sucking tube—except that the walls weren't made of water but mirrors. And in the mirrors' spinning she saw the warp of every single lie that she had ever told herself, every wasted moment, every stroke of self-deception. It was a giant, cone-shaped nullity. And she felt herself being sucked permanently into its pit.

She snapped her head back up and stood. She warmed the water and washed her face with cleanser. She dried herself and quickly applied light makeup. Her hair she put up with a clip. She gathered her things from the floor, deposited them in a hamper, went to her bedroom, put on her underwear, and dressed quickly in khakis, mules, and a sleeveless blue linen shirt. As she descended the main stairs, she flicked open her sunglasses and slipped them on.

In the foyer, the heavy front door stood partially open, something Sigrid could not abide. She would approach the garage from the outside, saving herself from a possible encounter in the kitchen with Tony. Again she felt rushes of despair. She grabbed the door's heavy brass handle as tightly as she could and shook it, as if shaking herself. She slammed the door behind her.

Outside, at the end of the flagstone walk, Tony and Caroline stood side by side, waiting for her. Behind them, parked in the circle, was the crouching midnight blue German station wagon, bigger, more elevated, bluer than it had been in her memory. It had a giant yellow ribbon on its hood. As Tony saw the expression on her face, his foolish grin melted into tears. Caroline clapped. Sigrid felt her legs wobble. It wasn't exactly the same car; she could see that it had the rims she had originally thought she wanted. There was a sunroof as well—something she hadn't even asked for. But the color was the same, and so was the interior.

"But what about Cissy Lord?" she asked, now fighting her own tears. "What about car pool?"

"We *planned* that, Mom," Caroline said, as if dismayed by her mother's gullibility. "You still have to take *me* to school."

"Happy birthday, Sigrid," Tony said, holding her around the shoulder, the way a doctor delivering bad news might. A sob escaped from behind her dark glasses. "You deserve this. You really do."

She kissed him quickly, not ready yet to forgive him for her emotions, and Caroline jumped happily with her book bag into the back seat. Sigrid walked around to the driver's side and climbed in, but then remembered the yellow bow, and got back out and plucked it off the roof and put it into the hatch at the back. Tony stood by, smiling widely. Back in the driver's seat, she again felt the electric tingle of the knobs and toggles, though she noted that the car did not have the more expensive stereo she had loved about the first one, and it had a few more miles on it than the version she had driven. Otherwise it was the same, but for a certain lesser feel. There was a sense that it was just a car—another car, rather than a different country or a new skin or a movie.

She pulled cautiously from the circle onto St. Dunstan's Way. She adjusted the mirrors, the seat back, the climate control, but didn't touch the radio. She drove up Charles to Northern Parkway, across Northern Parkway to Roland Avenue, and down Roland to take her place in the line of cars waiting to drop off. She pressed the button for the sunroof, and it retracted with military precision.

Beautiful, scrubbed-clean spring Baltimore sunlight flooded in, along with the fragrance of the blooming chestnuts that lined Roland Avenue. Caroline was watching out the window for her friends, who wouldn't know to look for her in a new car.

Cake

He says on the Monday evening after a decently successful dinner gathering Saturday, "Let's have a party this weekend; something, you know, to celebrate." "I've already gotten a sitter," Helen says. "Well, we could use the sitter. She could bathe and put the kids down for us while we entertained. We could invite, oh, perhaps, the Thompsons, the Wilsons, the Wexfords, the Channings." "It's our *anniversary*," Helen says. In fact, it is not their anniversary; however, for years they have agreed upon celebrating their anniversary on the second weekend of the month. "I know," he says, "that's why we're having an *anniversary* party." They are sitting on the back patio, beneath the striped market umbrella, though the late summer sun has disappeared behind the trees. He looks at his meal, a piece of grilled grouper and an ear of corn. "What if it rains?" Helen finally asks. "I can't have all those people in my house in the middle of August, period. It will be unmercifully hot outdoors, and it probably *will* rain, and I'll have a house full of people I didn't want to see in the first place on my anniversary." They sit in silence for a few moments. The mosquitoes are beginning to come out. "What did you have in mind?" he asks her. She says, "Maybe we could do something fun—like go see a movie and get a snack after, or I've been wanting to maybe visit the botanical gardens, where they are having an orchid show. They are open late on Saturdays in summer." "An orchid show?" he asks. "On our anniversary?" "It closes at the end of the month," she says. He takes his half-eaten plate and glass of wine inside and puts both into the kitchen sink and climbs the stairs, where he lies on the loveseat in the study in the dusk. An oscillating fan clicks as it twists on its old plastic track. He puts his forearm across his eyes and tries to sleep.

The following evening, Cassandra Bentley calls; Helen picks up the phone in the study. From their bedroom he can follow the conversation easily: The Bentley's have a ski condominium that they rent out year-round. However, the odd weekend will get canceled, leaving it free at the last minute; the Bentley's have been threatening for some time to invite them impromptu. For some reason, Helen wants to see the Bentleys' ski condo. He listens as she repeats Cassandra's invitation back to her, then the names of the other couple invited, the Wallops—people in their circle as well. He likes the Bentleys, and, in all honesty, has also been interested in seeing their mountain place. "Yes, yes of course," Helen says into the receiver to Cassandra Bentley. "It would be wonderful." "The Bentleys have invited us and the Wallops to Starwood for the weekend," she says when she's hung up with Cassandra Bentley. He stands for a moment in the doorway to the study. "I need to cancel the sitter," she says, picking up the telephone again. It reminds him of the story a couple told him at a party once. Just after marrying, the husband went into a bank and opened a joint checking account. That night, when he handed his wife her temporary bankcard, she asked, "What's the pin number?" "Our anniversary," he said. She said, "So: zero-seven-two-five?" He looked at her for a long time and then said: "I thought that would be too easy. I made it our anniversary plus a day."

They are in the condominium at Starwood on the second night. The parents are going to cook dinner in the big kitchen as soon as the children have finished their meals, bathed quickly, and jammied up. "What's that?" he asks Jim Bentley, his host. A cake is sitting on the counter. It's frosted elaborately in yellow cream, with what look like wedding ribbons in heavy folds on its top. "You guys brought it," Jim Bentley says. "I thought it was your anniversary cake. Don't you two always celebrate your anniversary on the second weekend of August?" Jim Bentley is holding a beer. They're both wearing shorts and flip-flops and their shirts hang tucked out. Jim Bentley hasn't shaved, and his cheeks are sunburned from the round of golf he and Tim Wallops had played that morning. Across the kitchen, Helen begins to cut the cake. She and the other two mothers distribute the small wedges of black and cream to the expectant children.

In the Woodlands

Ashley had been to Colonial Williamsburg before, both times staying with her parents at the luxury hotel with a piano that rose out of the floor at dinner. Jammy had visited as well, with his mother and grandmother—his father's mother—just after his father left them. They stayed in a motor lodge closer to Newport News than the Historic Area, on his grandmother's theory that anything within a reasonable distance of the attraction would be overpriced. He didn't have much recollection of the trip, other than fast-food meals in their room, stolen glimpses behind the doors of the houses as the more fortunate visitors slipped in—they hadn't bought tickets, but just wandered the area—and the souvenir wooden flintlock that his grandmother had bought him.

Ashley wouldn't stay at the Inn, the one with the piano, or the Lodge, for that matter, which was the less elaborate hotel across the street. She was trying to get away from "all that." Jammy got them a room at the Woodlands, a motel on the fringe of the Historic Area. It was still owned by Williamsburg—the furnishings were vaguely colonial, "Story of a Patriot" played on the television, and the room came with a copy of the Williamsburg gift catalogue. They had vigorous sex on one of the beds, showered, then walked to the Visitor's Center, where they stood in line to buy tickets. The

Freedom Pass was good for a year, which both of them considered inauspicious, and required a photograph. Ashley loved having her picture taken so much that she was standing in front of the digital camera before Jammy had even gotten his wallet out.

Outside the Visitor's Center, they boarded a bus, the city kind, but painted in somber gray and white, colors Jammy associated with reform schools and last-chance military academies. The driver was comically obese, and Ashley flirted with him as she boarded the striped steps, tossing her long blonde hair and shaking her shoulders so that the light white top she wore—not nearly enough cover for early morning in the retarded Virginia spring—shimmied. Ashley came from Charleston, South Carolina, and, until her Christmas vacation, had been a student at the infamous and exclusive Judge School there. Currently on an unannounced leave of absence, she still maintained some of that school's traditions, among them a certain flirtatious and neurotic way of dealing with all men, even the fat and slow. Though she and Jammy had been together for eight months, and full time for two, since leaving Charleston, she still rarely encountered a man, even with Jammy beside her, for whom she didn't pause, or so it seemed to Jammy, to be admired. Mainly, Jammy tolerated this—if she wanted to shake it for the fatty black bus driver, let her. Jammy came from a social class that, by virtue of being human racists, had no use for distinctions based on such fine gradations as skin color or ethnic origin. He didn't put people in classes. He hated them all.

They got off at the first stop in the Historic Area, along with a large, extended family of South Americans. Once the bus had lumbered on, they found themselves before an open shelter, which contained benches, a soda machine, and two women wearing long skirts. The women kept silver clickers in their aprons. They turned their floppy white-capped heads to and fro to ascertain that everyone getting off the bus had a badge. Ashley had hers pinned to the waist of her beltless blue jeans, in such a way that it drew even more attention to her peeking midriff. Under the watchful gaze of one of the women in shower caps, Jammy took his own badge from his back pocket and clipped it to a front one, a place, he thought, where it looked less like a damn uniform number. Ashley had her map out already, the brightly printed centerpiece of the colonial newspaper, which gave the day's date, though it was late March, as June 17, 1775. With the capped women, she planned their morning. Using an optic yellow highlighter, one of the women drew a looping route across the newsprint page, circling those things—the Governor's Palace, the Armory (for Jammy), the Statehouse—that were obligatory stops on the first turn through what she called "the Capitol." Meanwhile, the children of the South American family busily punched the soda machine in the shelter. Jammy felt hungry. Ashley thanked the woman, took Jammy by the hand, and led him to a rough-hewn wooden bridge that crossed a small stream. The stream's banks were busy with violets and Johnny-jump-ups. A wood-chip trail wound up into a wood and, as the map promised, their first visit.

In a small lane a fence that looked like drunks leaning against each other enclosed a half-acre plot. There was a small cabin on it. The morning air was moist and cool, and clotty smoke rose from the cabin chimney. A young black woman, again wearing an apron and a floppy cap, awaited them at a gap in the fence. As they approached, she positioned herself so that they wouldn't be able to slip by. Jammy sensed a lecture coming, a dose of instructive intelligence. It would be a tale whose moral would be how ungrateful he was for all that he had.

"The wealthy would have lived on the main street," she began. Ashley absent-mindedly fiddled with a button on her jeans as she dutifully received her introduction. "Already by this time, the rich property owners would have held nearly all the land in the Capitol, which they leased, such as we see here, to people who come in from the country to practice their trades." The woman gestured to the plot of land behind the fence. "The Commonwealth stretched to Ohio and Kentucky in those days, and the Capitol was the administrative center. As such it would be busy the year round. Plots such as these, on the byway, would rent for up to six months' worth of a tradesman's wages."

Having heard enough, Jammy slipped behind her, entering the uneven yard. Two long plots had been turned but not yet planted. For such a supposedly poor place, none of the usual farm junk lay about, tools dropped where last used or odds and ends piled where they might be good one day for something. In other words, it didn't resemble any small farm that Jammy knew of now or ever: Jammy seriously doubted that humans got tidier as they went back in time.

Near the cabin door a guy sat on a stump. He wore knee breeches, a frilly blouse, and a heavy brown jacket with wide lapels. He scraped awkwardly at a strip of wood stuck in a peg vice.

Ashley had caught up. "So, sir," she said to him. "What are you doing today?"

He didn't look up, but continued at his inept woodworking. He had shiny, smooth skin, wore small glasses, and was a little plump.

"*Hel-lo?*" she sang, doing one of her little "say-hey" shimmies, bending at the knees and jiggling her shoulders.

"I *very much* beg your pardon, Miss. Does it not occur to you that I am involved in a task of some utility and concentration?"

Ashley stepped back, though not nearly far enough for Jammy's taste, and assumed another of her poses, very erect, one hand on her hip, the opposite finger pressed to her full lips. "Apparently people in the eighteenth century didn't have a sense of humor," she said.

The guy returned to hacking at the plug of wood with his drawknife. "I am preparing a peg for Master Carter's clothes rack. His old peg has gone broken." The sun glinted in his small oval glasses. With another awkward swipe, he broke the peg in half, leaving a chunk of jagged pine.

About to laugh, Jammy mounted the cabin's two wooden steps and reached for the iron door handle.

The little man in breeches jumped from the stump he'd been

sitting on. "Excuse me!" he cried. "Do you enter another's house *unbidden?* This is my *home.*"

Startled, Jammy took a sudden step backward and then stumbled off the edge of the steps. By cartwheeling his arms he managed not to fall. Ashley laughed, then followed the whittler into his cabin. Jammy didn't immediately follow; he'd learned to control his anger that way. He studied the onion grass, which stood in tall clumps in the field. Just beyond the drunken-sailor fencing, a man in a brown work uniform turned the garden plot in the yard next door. A pale green pickup with a spreader in its bed sat in the lane. So it was an illusion after all. The clowns with the frilly shirts and weird glasses didn't do any of the real work. Everything here was maintained by the same guys who maintained everything else in the world—regular stiffs probably not even paid union scale.

There was another guy already inside the cabin, wearing the same baggy shirt and breeches. He stood before an ineptly built fire that smoked and sputtered. This was Master Carter. He had his own sob story: He was a poor clerk, struggling alone in search of his fortune, far from home. He made a production of sorting ragged-edged papers on a chest, all the while, it seemed to Jammy, staring at Ashley. When he had finished his moaning, the peg-maker started in again.

"As you can see," he said, "we live very plainly. In the summers, if it is not too hot, we throw open the windows. But in the winter, when the winds blow, even with every window sealed, it can become quite cold." He drew his hand across the small room, a droopy cuff dangling. "We live very simply."

Jesus fucking Christ, Jammy thought. With a fire like that, no shit you're cold. He walked into the next room—there were only two— and found a rope bed that was unmade. Three heavy axes and a thick billy club stood upright in a corner. This second room had an outside door as well, which was held closed by a wooden peg, neatly and evenly hewn, no doubt somewhere else, by somebody who actually knew about things like hand tools.

Jammy wanted to pick up the billy club and crack the two clowns in the next room on their heads. They were nothing more than a couple of faggy roommates like at some cushy college where people pawed books all day and beat off into the sheets. Jammy decided that he really *was* hungry.

"Come on, Ash," he yelled, pulling the smooth peg from the door and stepping out into the crisp spring air. After a moment, she followed.

Tail twitching and nut-brown eyes wide, face fur on end, the squirrel popped up the steps one at a time, then crossed the painted porch in sudden foot-long bursts until it crouched, quivering, eighteen inches from the morsel of ginger cake that Jammy held in his outstretched hand. The plainly tame rodent held its place, however, refusing to make the final advance, despite the inviting way Jammy gently floated the auburn cake, its top flecked with fat grains of sugar. The rodent, the master of twenty such encounters a day, acted well within the limits of its walnut brain: Jammy's boot, stretched out parallel with his arm, lay at quiet attention. It was Jammy's intention, at the moment of exchange, to slip the toe of his boot beneath the squirrel's furry belly and quickly flick it into a thick boxwood hedge. It was the way in which trust had been repaid his entire life.

Finally he lost patience and threw the piece of ginger cake into the courtyard below. The squirrel scampered back down to it, reaching the tidbit just before a sparrow, swooping from a bare tree above. Ashley was talking to a heavy middle-aged woman in a floppy white cap, multiple skirts, and an apron. She had planted herself uninvited on their bench with a heavy sigh. The woman was explaining indentured servitude in a faked accent. It was her opinion that a "fair young lady" of Ashley's station and age, "born well of manners and comeliness" should be busy at that moment stitching a piece of burlap with numbers, letters, and a pair of stick figures. Jammy took this to be a hardly casual comment on the disparity in their ages. Oftentimes Ashley wouldn't kiss him in public, and he feared that it was because his being so much older embarrassed her. He himself knew how people looked at them sometimes. He knew the look well. It was the look that said: "You are way out of bounds." It said: "You are looking for trouble, bub." She was seventeen—and only time was going to change that.

Jammy rattled the bag of ginger cakes; they'd bought a half-dozen of them. Ashley rose and thanked the woman kindly. The woman spread her hands and nodded her shower cap in Ashley's direction. Jammy followed Ashley down the porch steps. As he passed her, the woman said "Good day, kind sir."

"She's a different kind of person, Jammy," Ashley told him as they walked along the dirt lane, this time headed for the Governor's Palace. "It's interesting to talk to her. She has different experiences; she sees the world differently from us."

"But she's not a person, Ash. She's a character of a person who probably never existed. She's *made up.*"

"*Quit* it," she moaned, turning on him. "I hate it when you do that, criticizing the things I enjoy."

They walked in silence until they came to another stream, another bridge. The banks had greened over, and while the trees above resisted budding in the lingering winter, the low wet parts were verdant and alive. She took his hand again.

They decided against taking the Governor's Palace tour; it was forty-five minutes long and, fortunately, Ashley had only a short attention span for such things. In the courtyard scullery Jammy found himself looking at the food displays, large marbled hams and a big grilled fish covered in a milky glaze of lemon slices. The food was like paintings of food. The cook, a heavy pink woman who spoke in a reassuringly normal way, told him that it was all real and edible, if it wasn't left out the way it was, for days on end, until it dried up or began to smell. It didn't make Jammy hungry, exactly, but it fascinated him, the way meeting a pretty woman, but the kind of woman he'd never get with, fascinated him.

Next stop came the Robert Wilson House, complete with another scolding lecture on how hard people had it back in those days. It seemed pretty sweet, Jammy said to himself as she talked on and on to a small group trying to get in. Giant houses with plenty of food and servants. Finally she let the cluster of badge-wearing tourists pass into the garden. Everything was tiny and low, as if small people had built it. A horse stood in a corner stable, which the people took pictures of. The visitors moved in clumps of sneakers and windbreakers, their Freedom Passes pinned proudly to their chests. "Take a picture of the horse," a woman told her husband.

"Wait! Over here," Jammy said to Ashley within hearing range of the woman. "A blacksmith is pounding a red-hot piece of metal into something unrecognizable." In fact a bearded man wearing a heavy leather apron was whacking with a heavy hammer on a piece of metal. Everywhere Jammy looked he just saw fakery.

"Shut up, Jammy," Ashley said. Jammy put his hands into his pockets and followed behind.

The day was cold still and becoming cloudy. It looked like rain. They walked to the edge of the Historic Area and found a cafeteria where, along with about seven hundred Japanese, they ate bacon burgers and shared a cup of thrasher fries. The table's plastic seats were bolted to a wall. All during lunch Ashley kept looking over her hamburger across the room. She continued staring at such regular intervals that Jammy knew she was flirting. Crinkling his wrapper into a ball, he turned the next time she stared and saw a pretty boy with short dark hair and a leather jacket slumped in a booth by the window. He was drinking a Pepsi through a straw and smiling. He stopped smiling quickly, though, sat up in the laminated booth, and began talking with his two friends. Jammy had a criminal record, and some people, his grandmother, for example, claimed you could tell that from his eyes.

When they returned outside, the rain had begun to fall. In order to keep from getting soaked, they sneaked into the Williamsburg Inn, the place where Ashley had stayed with her mother and stepfather on her visits before. It looked to Jammy like pictures he'd seen of the White House. The main floor had long, tall hallways carpeted in wild interlocking designs. They paused at the door to the dining room—the room that Ashley said had the grand piano hidden beneath the floor. Starched white tablecloths, ranks of cutlery, upturned wineglasses, and small pots of flowers spread across the large room in a latticework design. Jammy looked in vain for the place in the floor from which the grand piano emerged.

"Let's go for it," he said to her on a whim. "Let's have our dinner here."

Ashley dragged him past the door and into the low-lit lobby, shooting him one of her sarcastic looks. Was it because he had the wrong clothes or wouldn't know how to behave? Indeed, the notion of eating with her in that kind of a place both scared him and filled him with an unfamiliar yearning. Why shouldn't his money be good there? The family of small South Americans was crowded into the lobby gift shop, where the women of the group wandered grimly from shelf to shelf, their arms full of creamware mugs, silver trivets, and flute-shaped glasses. Ashley pushed him past the gift shop and through the Inn's front doors, held open for them by a guy wearing brass buttons and a three-cornered hat. It was raining harder. The anger that Jammy could summon so easily began to simmer, clanking the flimsy aluminum lid that covered the cheap saucepot of his emotions. She didn't want to be seen with him—for her, he was just a phase, not somebody she loved. They marched silently to the shuttle bus stop and stood pressed together but not embracing beneath a small shelter while they waited. Ashley shivered and goosebumps rose on her arms. After a bit, the white-and-gray bus whooshed to a stop for them. It was the same fat driver who had picked them up earlier. This time Ashley ignored him. They rode the otherwise empty bus and Jammy tried calming himself. By the time they arrived back at the Visitor's Center, he had regained his poise. It was all about her stepdad, he told himself. Not about him.

They got into Jammy's car and Ashley directed them to a shop where they bought long, crusty bread and two different shapes of cheese. She also picked out grapes and a pear. A six-pack of beer from Germany. They took the food back to the room. This was dinner. How could these things together make dinner? But this was Ashley, and it was something that he was coming to love. After drinking a beer she lightened up and even got a little silly. She only weighed 110 pounds, after all. They brushed the crumbs from the bed, and began their usual sex—hot and frenzied kissing that transitioned unceremoniously into quick and mundane coupling. She was only seventeen, and sometimes it showed, but Jammy loved her.

While Ashley slept, Jammy drank the rest of the beer and watched a program on VH-1 about the 100 greatest rock songs of all time. He hardly recognized most of them. In between the songs by bands he'd never heard of, the program showed interviews with people—purported rock stars—whose identity he found similarly mysterious. They, in turn, all talked in reverential tones about people who were weirder sounding still. He wondered when rock, *fucking rock music*, had become another thing you had to take a college course to understand.

When Jammy woke, Ashley was seated on the sofa with the visitors' guides and yellow pages spread open on the coffee table in front of her. The Fox news played silently on the television. It was 10:30. She was dressed.

"Club Sources," she said, "sounds best." It intimidated Jammy the way Ashley dressed to go clubbing. She owned clothes from places he didn't even know existed and wore them in a way that was not revealing, exactly, but deeply tempting nevertheless. The effect was intended, Jammy couldn't help thinking, for someone else. He pulled on a pair of clean black jeans, retied his boots, and brushed his teeth before pulling on a black T-shirt that she had bought for him before they left Charleston.

Neither of them was good with directions and they didn't have a map. They drove in circles for a while through the dark wooded parkland of the Historic Area, where there were no streetlights. After nearly an hour of it, with Ashley becoming increasingly irate, Jammy glimpsed a gas station through the trees, a Texaco. They went there and he asked someone for directions at an all-night copy store next door. Club Sources turned out to be a fair distance, halfway to Newport News, along the road that Jammy remembered from his stay with his grandmother. They had the usual hassle at the door—Jammy looked dangerous and Ashley's fake I.D. was terrible—but finally the bouncer let them through.

"All for the pleasure of paying a five-dollar cover," Jammy said, throwing a ten at a girl with limp hair behind a glass counter. At the neon-lit bar, he ordered them each a kamikaze while Ashley went to the bathroom. Because she took so long—she always took an age in the bathroom—he drank hers, too, then ordered another one. Just then he was feeling blue, because he was thinking about his father. This was the trip they took after his father left. He and his mom and his grandmother. They never much went anywhere together ever again. There were pool tables in the back. Sooner or later, Ashley would want to dance. If he was playing pool, if he was winning, he wouldn't have to dance with her. He always felt awkward dancing in front of Ashley. She had high standards for dancing, or so she said, and was, of course, a really good dancer. In his mind, he imagined that when he wasn't around, she did a lot of it.

When Ashley got back from the ladies' there was a beer on the bar, but no Jammy. She looked toward the back, where the pool table was. He was bent over it, a pool cue flicking back and forth between his spread fingers as he readied his shot. In the opposite direction a kid sat by himself nursing a beer. She picked up her own beer.

"I know you," she said. He had round glasses and soft blond hair. He was wearing a wrinkled gingham shirt and chinos.

"I get that a lot," he said, sipping from his bottle.

"Oh, you do not," Ashley said. He was the guy who'd been whittling Master Carter's peg. "I bet it's never happened once."

He put down his beer and looked at her.

Across the club Jammy was holding the table until a fancy guy—belt, watch, faggy haircut—came up in the line. He took Jammy for a ride. Jammy didn't mind, exactly, because the kid was a smart player who took advantage of Jammy's mistakes. They played again and, concentrating, Jammy got him back. The kid, named Kevin, said that he worked at Williamsburg. That was when Jammy recognized him—he was one of the morons from the first house they visited, the one who cried about coming all the way from Hoochiecooch in search of his "fortune." Dressed more or less regularly he was an okay guy. He knew how to play pool. In some other world, he and Jammy might have been friends. So what if every day he wore breeches and a frilled shirt and said shit like *we live very simply?* It was just a job. Jammy's father had taught him to hate fancy people—guys in suits with shiny shoes and platinum watches. But also he taught him to respect a working man, no matter what he did.

At very nearly the same moment, Ashley was getting Rick's story: He was from Charlottesville but had gone to college in Williamsburg.

"I did English and creative writing at W and M," he told her, moving closer. He'd been working at Williamsburg since he graduated. He had gotten his roommate a job there, too, which was cool, because they worked together. When people weren't around, which was most of the time, because they were assigned to basically the stupidest of the houses, they just hung out. Ashley drew her hair behind an ear and nodded. "My band just broke up," he went on. "We were really good. But our drummer had to go to pharmacy school."

"That's such a drag," Ashley said.

"I write all my own stuff. It's going to work out, but not here." He waved his beer. "This place is all about classic rock and country. Never anything really good," he said. "Whatever."

He asked her if she wanted to get some cigarettes with him, and she agreed. They went out into the parking lot to his car and drove across the street to a gas station. Rick got some cigarettes while Ashley watched the reflection of the gasoline pumps as they jiggled in the puddles of water on the ground. They drove back to the Sources parking lot and she let him kiss her. She kissed him back hard.

Jammy was so fucked-up that Ashley had to drive back to the Woodlands. She wasn't in great shape herself, but she'd spent enough time with Rick for the two beers she'd had to mellow a little. Fortunately, Rick and Kevin left around the same time, and she followed them. She felt a little bad doing that to Jammy—getting directions from a guy she had just hooked up with—but it was his fault for getting blitzed, after all. Rick led them right to the motel parking lot, and both guys waved to her before circling out of the lot and speeding into the night and away. She lugged Jammy to the room, gripping him by the belt loops of his black jeans. Once he saw where they were, he wanted to make it, but he couldn't get his pants off, even. After a short time, thankfully, he passed out crosswise on one of the beds.

When Jammy woke at dawn the next morning, his first thought was of his father. Of the way it was before he left for good. And then he thought with regret about having come to Colonial Williamsburg. He was sorry he drank so much; he was sorry he had to be such a fucking idiot. He got up and touched Ashley, sleeping beneath the sheets on the next bed. She was so skinny that, when she lay that way, on her side, she looked like a snake that'd swallowed a rat. She woke to his touch and said, "I love you." She almost never said that. They made love.

After three cups of coffee and a sticky cinnamon bun from the Burger King nearby, Jammy took a last look around the room. It was actually pretty nice. It had historic-looking furniture and a parquet floor near the door and a nice carpet otherwise. The television was hidden in a honey-colored cabinet, the towels were plush, the pillows soft, and the bedspreads were crisp and pretty. There were wooden blinds in the windows. How much nicer could it have been? He thought about how Ashley, despite being temperamental and often childish and a flirt and generally sometimes a pain in his ass, did show him better things—crusty bread and funny cheeses—and take him better places. She was a lot younger than he was, but she, too, was teaching him things. She was making him better.

As he looked to see if he'd left any of his socks beneath chairs, his eye fell on the Colonial Williamsburg gift catalogue. Ashley had been looking at it while lying on the couch and waiting for him to get ready. On the cover was a photograph of a pudgy little guy dressed in breeches and a jacket, sitting cross-legged and staring dreamily out a window. Jammy recognized him. He was the roommate from the night before—the dip who didn't know how to whittle.

Dan, Astrid Says

"Dan," Astrid says, "didn't I tell you this story? About Burton Kelly sitting next to Tim Judge at a restaurant in Rio de Janeiro?" Realizing her mistake—this is a tender issue—she turns to the other guests at the table and continues with her story. Burton Kelly, a journalist friend from Washington, went to Rio to visit his girlfriend or a friend of his girlfriend, or something like that. This friend, as it turns out, knew Tim Judge, finishing at SAIS, also in D.C. "Remember," she addresses a woman at the opposite end of the table, Rima, the only woman she knew when she first moved to Las Vegas, "we went to a party with him and Polly Watson and Kira and some other people last summer?" The woman nods and takes a sip of wine. Astrid returns to her story. "Tim Judge and Burton Kelly end up sitting together at a dinner party held in a restaurant in Rio. Burton introduces himself to Tim, and vice versa, and Burton says he's a journalist with *Smithsonian*. And Tim says, hey, do you know Astrid Wright? Of course, Burton says, I do. Do *you* know Astrid Wright? Well obviously he does. Isn't that wild? At a restaurant in Rio?

Curt, who sits next to Rima across the table, speaks up: "Wait— how did you know these people?" And Astrid explains about writing a feature for *Smithsonian* over a year before; it was her first cover. Judge she knows, she says, from . . . "Well, Rima, how *do* we know Tim Judge?" Marta, their hostess for the evening, stands and brings a plate of Norwegian cookies and brews coffee for the few who are having it. Curt pours himself some more wine, then passes the bottle down to Dan. Curt's roommate, Josh, is falling asleep. In a lull over the cookies, Josh wakes. "What?" he asks, as everyone at the table is looking at him. "I wasn't sleeping."

In the courtyard when Dan and Astrid leave the pool lights are on and the water shimmers as if someone had recently slipped from it. Astrid stops and puts her arms around him. It is a clear, hot night and the courtyard palmettos riffle. The sky above the balconies and stucco façades is black; the city light, sulphurous orange, erases the stars.

"I love you," she says. "I love it that you're here." Dan holds her. Black-capped garden lights illuminate the winding path, the condo trail. This whole complex, a spread of three city blocks of redevelopment in salmon and tan, its railing a pale sage, still possesses all the accouterments of suburban renting. The automatic misters snap on, frilling the settled water.

"Burton Kelly," he says. "Back in the picture?" Astrid goes limp in his arms and moans. He holds onto her. "I'm serious," he says. "Is that what's going on?"

"No," she says, twisting away from him and walking a few paces ahead along the winding path. He follows her and takes her hand. They enter the gate, again, pale sage, and walk to the edge of the pool. The misters catch small rainbows in the air. "He e-mailed me to say he'd met someone who knew me in Rio. So I e-mailed Tim Judge and asked him what in the hell was up with that. I didn't even know that Tim was down there."

"So," Dan says, "You and Burton Kelly are e-mailers?"

"*No*," she says again, lifting his hand in hers then throwing it down again, in emphasis. "He sent me a long piece he'd written, that he'd been working on for a long time. I read it and called him and told him I liked it, which I didn't really. That is to say, his writing is fine, but, you know, he's a journalist, and after a certain point there's no variation in his style and it becomes annoying. So I got on the phone and said, hey, I liked the piece, and he said, oh, thanks, and I said, okay, is Paul Weller there? And he transferred me. That's all. Don't be jealous about it. Please. Don't."

"Don't I have some reason for being concerned?" he says. "Can't you see why I'd be concerned?"

"Please, please, please," she says.

Though it's well after midnight, it is still quite hot; the desert air hangs in stacks over them, as if so much dry atmosphere exerts more pressure on their skin, not less. There is no lightness in the evening, none of night's light coat. The misters switch off and the last of the water's fine gauze drifts to the surface of the pool.

"Listen," she says. "Why am I in trouble for this? What did I do wrong? He's still an editor, he still knows everybody in the world. It would be senseless to drop him entirely, to ignore him. You know that. You do, right? He called me, not even called, e-mailed me in the spring saying he was going through town, could we get together? I told him, didn't tell, wrote him, you know, Sorry, I'm out that night. What did I do wrong? See there's nothing for you to worry about. Do you believe me? Okay? I shouldn't have brought it up, I know. It was just such a good story."

They embrace again, turn, walk arm in arm through the pale gate outside the pool enclosure, past the mailboxes, across a quiet street, and to the open-air vestibule of Astrid's building. By pressing a gray bauble that hangs from her key chain to a matte black box, the pale sage gate that leads to her courtyard clicks. She pushes it open. The elevator bell dings, echoing off the salmon-colored nubbly walls. They ride to the fourth floor and walk together down the open hallway, ceiling fans turning lazily overhead in the breeze-less heat.

"Aren't you glad you met them?" she asks, meaning her new friends Marta and Curt and Josh and Rima Brookhardt, the person she knew when she first came to Las Vegas. They stand for half an hour in her kitchen and she tells him more about each of them, now that he knows them.

The next day on the plane, she sits by the window. Across her lap spreads the Mojave, cracked and broken, with its endearing Joshua trees and persistent creosote bushes. He's never met Burton Kelly, though once he saw a photograph. Before Burton Kelly there had been one other, but he didn't know his name. He has come to regard them as casualties: victims of the glacier, heartbreaking-blue and shockingly crevassed, that he now traverses. Dan hasn't seen Burton Kelly's long piece; he doesn't read *Smithsonian*. Perhaps it's on something like creosote bushes, giant fairy rings in Michigan, or, maybe, some Swiss glacial moraine, disgorging the last century's lost and forgotten dead. That's the sort of thing *Smithsonian* reports on. Probably he isn't a very good writer. In the photograph that Dan saw he was short, shorter than Astrid. She had her arm around him, and they were standing in a cubicle at the magazine, probably his, both smiling. He wore a goatee. It left an offensive swelling around Astrid's mouth, and two red welts, like a downturned smile, upon her lower lip. They—the welts—faded painfully slowly to Dan's liking, as Astrid's pale skin healed at a glacier's pace. It has been seven months. In the welts' place appeared two tiny asterisms of fair freckles that Dan still locates easily when close to her, marking her as if to never allow him to forget.

The flight attendant, a blonde dressed in a blue smock that ties at the front, hands them trays of food: a salad with razor blades of lettuce and deathly cold strips of chemically cooked chicken. Astrid looks at her food and makes a face. They unwrap their plastic utensils and look again back out the window. Mexico lies across the hazy yellow horizon. She wants to go there and find a piece. Dan thinks that she is a splendid writer. She has a formula sometimes, which he has discerned, but it is a formula that works. It's in her endings, which, rather than wrapping up the matters at hand, invariably *wrap around*, bringing the reader, as if by promise fulfilled, to some place, some detail, or some person she has introduced earlier, but never entirely balanced the books on. In her money pieces, written half a dozen times a year for travel magazines and women's interest, she is explicit. *"And whatever happened to Rodrigo? Well . . . "* Or, *"Mr. Sandoz arrives at the hotel early on the morning of my last day in Lubjliana."* In her more complex pieces—her best ones—she leaves her conclusion as a puzzle. The reader ends the piece himself, by understanding at last the point she is making.

The beverage cart arrives and he buys them each an airplane bottle of white wine. He's not feeling himself; they've been cheating sleep on this trip, and he drank too much of the wine, even if it was only Riesling, that Curt poured at Marta's. He cracks the top, pours it out into the plastic tumbler, and drinks it like medicine. The altitude makes his head ache, and the glare on the insulated glass hurts his eyes. He takes Astrid's hand. *I shouldn't have brought it up. It was just such a good story.* But why? Because two strangers who had an acquaintance in common were seated next to each other at a café in Rio? Why? She isn't that naive a storyteller, even when narrating for her new, somewhat plain Las Vegas friends, a lawyer, someone in marketing, another journalist. In fact, her stories tend to be so sophisticated that she sometimes perplexes him painfully; she is the single person in his life who confounds him. The way she dresses, how she walks, the wizardry with which she writes, her wildly alternating moods, conveyed over the phone when they're apart, which is usually, when she's in the middle of something. The way she is in bed. The way she shaves her legs in the shower, the ritual with which she washes her hair. He loves her, he thinks, but is left fretful by the way she eludes his understanding. She intimidates him. In many ways, he hates it that he loves her, that he is trapped without ropes in the middle of her broad glacier, behind him no return, ahead no refuge. He hates it that he has learned how to read her stories.

Better never to begin. If you must begin, better to finish quickly.

Dan slips further into the Airbus seat, until he can feel its aluminum frame at his shoulder blades, beneath his thighs. He pushes the salad away to the extent he is able. Fatigue, hangover, the morning's stolen nacreous secretions float lazily through his head. Why else would it have been a good story? Two men are seated at a table, an outdoor restaurant, sea salt on the table, the smell of sweet cassava and coconut milk in the air.

The bell signaling descent rings in the cabin. *Dan, didn't I tell you this story?*

No wood without bark.

The plane drifts out over the Pacific, past the university, then curls back in its wood-shavings approach to the slim strip of Santa Barbara airport. At the moment of touchdown the sun glints through the cabin. They climb down the gangway while khaki-shorted youths, deeply tanned, their orange sound bafflers hanging around their necks, convivially direct the way to the low, tile-roofed terminal. The air is so rich, fragrant, and cool, vegetal rather than mineral. When Dan emerges from the restroom, Astrid stands, flipping through a magazine she has found at the newsstand in the small lobby.

"I *got* it," she says when he reaches her. "He let me have it. Or didn't notice it. But I got it. It went through!" The pages of the thick, glossy magazine droop from her hand like the leaves of some exotic garden tropical. The blown-in subscription inserts lie unminded at her feet. She's checked her lead, the piece's art and decks, and what her editor has done with cutlines. She doesn't let Dan see her pieces anymore before they go to press, unless she's strayed off into an odd or specialized subject on which she requires reassurance. He's okay with that; she doesn't need him poking at her copy. He will read the piece when he has the chance, in front of her or near her, as she prefers. Though she is preternaturally serious about her writing, she takes an adorable pleasure in having the particularly clever parts—the ingenious turn of phrase, the absurdly utile description, or the cruelly indicting detail pointed out. It is as if they play a game, where she salts even her most casual pieces with tiny nuggets of inside reference, always homogenous with the surrounding rock, but nevertheless extrinsic, for him alone. Or for him—as she is an artist and an intellect—and anyone else clever enough and patient enough to receive the favors that she holds in her cool blue depths.

At the car counter they are presented with the standard proffer: For a few dollars more a day they might have a convertible rather than whatever pumpkin seed of a car it is that Astrid has reserved. "Is it *red?*" she asks the young woman behind the counter, also pretty, blonde, and tanned, as if the Santa Barbara airport has taken seriously its mission of serving as the filmed illusion of an airport, rather than the thing itself.

"I don't know if this specific one is red, it doesn't say, but we may possibly have a red one on the lot." They take the convertible—white after all. "Why didn't you order a convertible?" Dan asks her in the lot. She smiles. "I should have." They put their bags in the trunk and sit in the deep bucket seats to watch the retracting lid. They make it to Ojai in less than forty-five minutes of climb and wind through dusty chaparral, which gives way in unexpected bursts to groves of almonds and oranges. The orange trees, particularly, are tucked tightly into impossible contours, clinging to the lips of the folded hillsides.

Astrid unpacks the few things—mineral water, a bottle of wine, some Gorgonzola and crackers—that they bought at a grocery outside Santa Barbara before turning inland. A knock comes at the door. Dan answers.

"We're here," Peter Mooney says, handing over a dusty bottle, something from his cellar. Over Peter's shoulder and across the motor court, Dan can see Erica, his wife, tall and distinctive in her blonde pageboy, resolutely ferrying vintage luggage from the trunk of their Mercedes to their room. Peter and Dan hug in the doorway.

It is significant that Erica hasn't joined him. Dan knows that she has come for a glimpse of Astrid, who, while both craving this moment and dreading it, has chosen to remain out of sight, in the unit's small, sour-smelling kitchen. Now faced finally with the moment of introduction, Dan has forgotten the way in which he had planned to do it. The motor court has become busier. People shuffle back and forth from open car trunks to motel room doors. Dan recognizes none of them, though they must all be there for Chris Wedin's wedding. Wedin is an artist in Pasadena, and the people who are arriving look as if they've made the drive in from Los Angeles for the rehearsal dinner. One woman, wearing a dove-gray duster, wanders down the breezeway reading room numbers. At its end, the court opens onto a small swimming pool surrounded by chain link. Beyond that two ponies drink from a low black plastic tub behind a barbed-wire fence. Past the corral a line of low dusty trees edges a stream. Across the stream a grassy flood plain gives way to another orange grove running up into the sudden rough foothills of the Ojai valley. It is a pretty, late-fall afternoon, and the outside air carries on it the faint smell of a stale corridor. Perhaps it is the ponies, or the grassy flood plain beyond. The chaparral and eucalyptus smell that way as well.

"Peter!" Erica calls out from across the court, not quite in a bark, but with her voice carrying. She slams the trunk of the car.

"See you at six?" Peter asks.

Chris Wedin and Cornelia, his fiancée, have chosen a mariachi band to play at their rehearsal dinner. The band members wear matching gold embroidered trousers and short jackets. The player of the *guitarrón* is so fat that he's busting from his pants. With his dark, single-quotes mustache he looks exactly like Gordo from the comic strip. The dinner is being held beneath a tent, during the installation of which, earlier that afternoon, the roustabouts had ruptured a water main. Chris has been on the scene since, negotiating the wedding's first disaster, and he greets Dan and Astrid in a dirty Carhart jacket, two-day's growth of beard, and jeans dried with mud. This time there is no explaining to do, because there is no time. Chris is as gracious to Astrid as if he'd known her his entire life. The band plays; a woman in a Mexican wedding dress ladles margaritas from a giant ribbed-glass jar in the dusk. Small lanterns hang in the trees. The wedding planner, frayed thin already by the water mishap, seizes the band's microphone and begs the guests to begin the buffet. Dan and Astrid join the line to the tables of hammered steaks and *posole* and tamales and a chile stew. It moves slowly. Peter and Erica join behind them.

"Why am I here?" Peter asks Dan.

Everyone wears nametags. "Hi," says Dan to the couple standing before him. "I'm Dan Andrews." Behind him, Astrid is attempting conversation with Erica Mooney. It has been agreed upon already that she will never become Astrid Andrews.

"We know who you are," says the husband. His wife, darkly beautiful, stands firmly beside him. "We were college roommates of Chris's. We inherited him from you."

Astrid provides Erica with skeletal details: Las Vegas, the story she is working on, and the one in the magazine that she's just picked up at the airport. For an awkward moment it becomes clear that the attention of all five of them—Erica, Peter, and the couple from Chris's college—hang on what Astrid is saying. But the line moves. The couple ahead must turn to lift their colored plates. Mexican women with ridiculously long spoons turn the contents of the chafing dishes. At that moment, Chris Wedin appears for the second time, showered and shaved, in boots and fresh jeans. Women have always loved Chris Wedin: tall, sandy blonde, laconic, and nice to a fault. Now Dan watches as he talks with Astrid and she smiles and then laughs out loud. When they are together alone, she is so often serious; seeing her with others, other men, particularly, sends a lonely shiver through him.

Later, when they are in bed, in the dark stillness of the paneled motel room, she says, "I wish *I* were marrying Chris Wedin. He's *lovely.*"

The next morning after breakfast Dan and Astrid ride with Peter and Erica in the Mercedes to a trailhead in the foothills east of town. It will be an evening wedding; they have the day to kill. Erica has still not spoken to Dan or made eye contact with him, even. However, they were barely on speaking terms to begin with. She wears conspicuously expensive sunglasses and rests her head against the Mercedes's side window. Bearing three children has softened her somewhat, but her jaw and cheekbones still maintain their firm resolution, as if her father had been a military officer, which he was, a marine aviator, in Vietnam. The bright sunlight on her hair highlights the strands of color-resistant gray, mellow as the fawn leather she lies languidly against. She lifts a finger from where it has rested against her lips and points, a subtle but unmistaken gesture, to an old taupe Volvo. It is the only other car parked at the side of the road near the trailhead.

Peter parks beside the old Volvo and the four of them begin to hike, along an old road skirting the valley wall that, after the requisite number of wash-aways, has been converted to a gentle footpath.

"If Gore wins," Peter says, "I'm afraid of a national crisis of confidence. I like the guy myself. However, as president, I think that he would be worse than Carter. I think he'd plunge the country into a funk."

Dan pulls an orange from one of the dusty trees that hang over the trail. Erica and Astrid walk ahead, laughing. In fact, there is no reason why Erica should not like Astrid.

"Why in hell doesn't Gore claim the high ground on inheritance tax?" Dan asks, peeling his orange. "And argue for a significant increase in the ceiling—protect the family farmer, say—and yet mobilize the traditional Democratic base by standing steadfast against tax breaks for the wealthiest?"

"Clinton would do it," Peter says. "Gore has polluted his politics with the personalities of his own social class. His peer group is made up of wealthy, liberal capitalists. Thus he's afraid to demonize them, he's afraid of offending them for his own political gain, even if just by practicing demagoguery. Clinton would never have had that problem."

"What about Clinton?" Dan asks. "In your opinion, if Gore can win with Clinton, but refuses to use him on moral grounds, does one respect Gore for risking his presidency on principle, or, conversely, do we condemn him for sacrificing his candidacy for his own, after all arguable, mores?"

"Either way," Peter says, "without Clinton, next week Gore loses."

The wedding is held at a bird preserve down the valley. The couple are married beneath a bower woven with blue and white flowers, a subtle allusion to the fact that Cornelia's mother is, though it's largely unknown, Jewish. The ceremony itself is a variety of homespun Lutheran, delivered by the pastor of the Colorado church to which Dr. and Mrs. Wedin belong. Cornelia's four bridesmaids, strung like a glossy archipelago upon the grass, are beautiful and distant. All tall, thin, and icily gorgeous women, judging from their expressions, they are in equal parts repelled to be wearing matching dresses and glorious to be standing with flowers in their hair in the sun. Chris whispers through his vows; Cornelia, just a few years younger, speaks more quietly still. From the second row, even, Dan can see only the movement of her bare shoulders as she repeats the pastor's words. Large cages full of injured raptors lie just beyond the party grounds, and birdhouse sounds, the plumping of feathers, the changing of feet, the stretching of wings, the hooding of eyes, fill the quiet mountain air. The pastor, using both hands, turns the couple to face the crowd. He raises his arms. The audience, wobbling in white folding chairs on the uneven, sloped turf, applauds. Dan turns to Astrid and she, utterly dry-eyed, smiles.

The reception begins with a clanking parade of Asian-inflected hors d'oeuvres. In the jumble, around the tables on the crowded lawn, the darkly beautiful college friend of Wedin's appears beside Dan and sits in the chair vacated moments before by Astrid. "We've recently moved to Seattle," she says. "My husband is a writer. He is looking for work."

"Seattle," Dan says. "Have you been there long enough to begin thinking of killing yourself yet?"

She meets his eyes. "That was in Portland," she says, laughing, but holding his eye in such a way that he knows—they both know—that she means it. "I've recently taken a job designing catalogues for Nordstrom," she says. "Not as bad as one would think."

"I like Nordstrom," Dan says. "I have a personal shopper there. It's remarkable, really. She picks out my ties; she sends me shirts when I need new ones. She calls me and tells me to come try on a jacket and I do and usually I buy it. It's like a story in a book, but it works."

"We really did inherit him from you," she says. "We were freshmen in college, and he missed his home so much. He missed you. I wanted to see you, to try and understand what you could have done to him to make him that way."

"I remember we wrote a lot of letters back and forth then," Dan says.

"I read all your letters."

"Where are you from?" Erica asks from across the table. Dan has forgotten she is there. Peter has left the table as well.

"Seattle," the woman says. Being with these people makes Dan feel as if he were nineteen again. He wonders where Astrid is.

"Do you have any children?" Erica asks, placing an elbow on the white tablecloth and leaning forward in a way that's nearly aggressive. The woman shakes her head quickly and says no. Her dark hair drifts into her face. Dan can see that she is beginning to cry.

When the toasts start, Cornelia and Chris, making their rounds, are caught at Dan and Astrid's table. Cornelia, overwhelmed by her organza and illusion, looks as if she might sink. Some New York cousins talk as a group. Then her brother, a Ph.D. candidate in the history of consciousness at UC Santa Cruz, gives a complicated, barely cogent speech. Chris's younger brother, a hunting guide when he's working, takes the microphone next, starts to cry, stops, starts to cry again, then gives up with a wave of the hand. Next comes the husband of one of Cornelia's cousins, a handsome North Carolinian, who, in his mind at least, is speaking for one side of the family. Already drunk, he becomes instantly raunchy. Cornelia tugs at the sleeve of Dan's jacket.

"Get up there," she says. "Say something. Take the microphone out of his hand and say something." Dan tries not to look at her. "Go!" she whispers, pushing at his back. Somewhere over the years, in the back of his mind, he'd been saving a wedding toast for Chris Wedin. But the time has passed. He doesn't have the first idea of what to say. Cornelia's father rises, takes the microphone from the drunken cousin, and Cornelia and Chris are called to the dais.

Peter drives the four of them back to the motel in the black Mercedes. "I have no idea why I was invited," he says. "I have no idea why I came."

"Dan was invited," Erica says, as if he weren't in the car with them. "You and Chris are friends."

Peter begins to say something, but arrests the thought. Dan knows that Peter and Chris Wedin never were particularly close. Peter's invitation was a courtesy only. And in reality Peter came to Ojai to see Astrid, to look at her. Dan had meant to tell him more before they arrived, to prepare his friend better, but in the rush and confusion, in the vortex his life has become, he never found the right time. And now that they are finally together, the whole weekend has begun to sound like a mariachi band of broken strings and busted trumpet valves.

"You know, I think I've gotten drunk and sobered up twice already tonight," Peter says. Dan studies his profile in the flicking Ojai streetlights. He knows that Peter hadn't wanted a third child, a third daughter as it turned out, now eighteen months old. Erica had insisted. Thin and handsome, with Kennedyesque dark hair, in the flicking blue light Peter looks tired. Friends since early childhood, Dan can no longer deny that they are becoming old.

At 3 A.M., still stranded on eastern daylight time, Dan rises, dresses quietly, takes his keys, and walks out into the motor court. The woman in the dove-gray duster sits in a plastic chair by the pool, talking quietly with two men Dan also recognizes from the wedding. A fog is creeping up from the riverbed, and he can just make out the forms of the ponies, very still and with their necks bent to the ground. He turns and crosses the motor court until he comes to the main street, which he follows toward town's central Spanish-style arcades. All the stoplights flash. Not even the Sunday papers have arrived. The blue fog becomes heavier, then begins to produce tiny flecks of rain. *Dan, didn't I tell you this story?* He comes to a darkened grocery story and looks through its tall windows. On one of the check-out conveyors a box of crackers, a bottle of fruit juice, and a pack of family napkins all sit neatly, as if one last customer had gone unchecked before closing. *It was just such a good story.*

Think that all phenomena are like dreams.

When the getaway brunch begins it has begun to rain terrifically hard. Hung-over wedding guests huddled beneath golf umbrellas splash down a lane strewn with fallen eucalyptus leaves. Champagne and orange juice, strawberries and fat muffins lay on a heavy table with thick, scrolled legs. The guests, as subdued as the day, stand in clumps and watch as the rain pours off the lip of the roof. Inside, Dan and Astrid separate, and in just the moment that he's been apart from her, Erica Mooney pinions him between a gaily painted armoire and a stuccoed wall. She carries a teacup and a cranberry muffin, its crown asparkle with thick flecks of sugar, balanced on the saucer.

"So, Dan," she says, using his name as if to underline that she hasn't spoken it once all weekend. "Do you travel much?"

He laughs; it's involuntary, but natural. It hurts no more than a slip on the ice.

"Don't laugh, you bastard," she says to him, fixing his eyes with hers. "You know what? I think you're a bastard. I hate you. I want you to know that. I hate your fucking guts."

With no more warning that a flash of rose scent, Chris Wedin's mother appears at Dan's side.

"Hello, there," she says to them. "It was wonderful to see you both last night." Dan cannot bring himself to look at Erica, to see if she has registered any embarrassment over what was certainly overheard. "You know," Mrs. Wedin goes on, now addressing Dan alone. "Of course, Chris tells us so much about you. But let me ask you something. Last night, after we got back to the hotel, when I'd gone to bed, just before falling asleep, something struck me. It occurred to me that you must have a child with red hair."

Dan regards her for a moment. The rain pours down on the tiled roof above. He has not seen Mrs. Wedin since he left for college; even then she was barely more than a voice on the telephone, or a small woman in an apron forever in the kitchen at the back of the Wedin's house.

"I do," Dan replies finally. "I have a son with red hair. His hair is quite red, in fact. Unmistakably so. He turned five just this month."

"I knew," she says. "It's funny. With everything else that was going on, for that to come to mind. But it did, as I lay there, it came to me. I saw it. As clear as day. Your redheaded son."

Rain: California rain; apocalyptic rain; endlike rain.

Shortly thereafter, Dan and Astrid drive in their drafty convertible to their room with the knotty pine walls. Peter and Erica have left straight from the brunch for the drive back to San Francisco. Most all the other wedding guests are checking out as well. In the vacated rooms, their doors propped open, each television set blares with the same Mexican soccer match. Dan and Astrid pack the remainder of their things. Tonight they will spend an extra night in Santa Barbara, so that Dan can eat in a restaurant he's read of there. "What do you want to do with this?" she asks, holding the dusty bottle of wine that Peter brought. The next morning Astrid will return to Las Vegas and Dan to Baltimore. When Astrid's bag is packed, she looks under the bed and behind the bathroom door for a second time. He studies her as she moves about the room: dramatically prepossessing, impossibly self-confident. Even in the quotidian fear of leaving some garment behind, she remains distant and mysterious. *Dan, didn't I tell you?* The confession about her affair with Burton Kelly—really, just a few nights in February—came in

June. When she told him, she confessed to one other such occurrence, during the autumn before. She wanted it to be entirely clear. At that point they came to an arrangement; it wouldn't happen again. Thus resolved, the memory became simply collateral damage. Dan does his best to ignore the wreckage. When that is impossible, he stares at it directly, clearing everything from his mind, like a monk in the charnel ground. Such moments of meditation are inescapable. Now he has a second corpse in the ice to coolly contemplate. *It was just such a good story:* Tim Judge, in a restaurant in Rio. What on earth are the odds? His twisted figure, lying frozen on the glassy blue surface of the glacier a few yards beyond Burton Kelly's, is the nugget that she had left in the story, just for him.

Alfalfa Valve

Andy Furlong is visiting his parents for the week, standing in the kitchen, looking at his mother's new phone. It's a home-office model, with a fourteen-station speed-dial. She hasn't written in any names on the template—she wouldn't—but he suspects that she has programmed them. From a childish impulse, part curiosity, part mischievousness, he lifts the handset and touches the first station. He lives a good distance—thousands of miles—away and feels that by rights the first number stored should be his; hers, that is, his parents', is first on his own. He pushes the button. But rather than the rip of quickly tumbling electronic beeps, a cascade through the fourteen digits he expects, the dial breaks off, as if only fitfully programmed. Almost immediately, there's an answer.

"Zebulon emergency services," says a woman in a calm and serious voice.

He hangs up. He remains by the telephone guiltily. He should have stayed on the line to explain.

The telephone rings and he answers it.

"This is emergency services. Did you just call?"

He's relieved, really. Or course they know that he called, or that his number called: all this is recorded, obviously. Now he has a chance to explain.

"I did. That is, I did dial you, but by accident. Hit the wrong speed-dial; though, of course, why my mother needs your number —just three digits after all—on speed-dial, which requires itself two digits, is utterly beyond me. Which explains, to begin, you see, part of my confusion. You answered, I guess, just as I was hanging up."

There's a studied pause.

"Is this Lawrence Furlong?" she asks. That's the next awkward thing. Everyone calls his father Law; since he was a child he's hated the name Lawrence. Consequently, Lawrence is so foreign a name, even to his son, that Andy pauses a moment, inadvertently. Like, "Who's Lawrence?"

"No," he says. "Not actually. I'm at his house; I'm his son, Andy. Andy Furlong, of course. Dr. Furlong, in fact, since this is emergency services."

Another studied pause hangs. "Is Mr. Furlong there, in the house? Or Mrs. Furlong either, Anne Furlong?"

Again, his mother is Nan, never Anne. Neither of his parents can bear their given names, for whatever ridiculous reason, because they're both quite plain names. This time he doesn't hesitate.

"Lawrence, Law, actually he goes by—that also proves I'm family, and not just saying that—is here, but he's asleep. He's old, well, older, I think I should say, because he is in good shape, but he's a napper. Actually, he's always been one. Ever since I was small, I can remember the naps. The siesta. As it turns out, if you follow the literature, I'm a doctor, a physician, you see, an internist, in fact, naps aren't very good for you. They disrupt your normal sleep cycle. For once our Puritan forebears were right about something, I guess. Anyway, he's napping, or I'd put him on right now, let him clear the whole matter up for you."

He hears from her end a squelch, the console next to the one he speaks with, he assumes, ringing off. Fire, robbery, escaped cow: Zebulon, though it has grown unbelievably in the past ten years, is surrounded still by the agricultural. He imagines the woman he speaks to sitting at a glowing console, computer screen, bank of phones, detailed book of maps, emergency-procedure loose-leaf (in red, of course) tidily arranged on the desk in front of her. In January—now it's June—he'd been on jury duty in Towson, Baltimore County, in Maryland, where he lives. It was one day only, and he was never called. He wandered around the courthouse. The county's emergency services center—it probably had an inflated name: Co-ordinated Action Response Detail, or Catastrophe Alleviation Readiness Department, thus CARD, so the county executive could get on television in times of disaster and say "The CARD was there"—lay in the basement. He spent part of his lunch break watching from the observation deck, which was really just a glassed passage leading to the cafeteria. He found it interesting. He'd never really considered that aspect of it.

"Is everything all right there?" she asks.

He finds himself a little frustrated by the question: after all, hasn't he put himself out already to explain to her the circum-stances? He recognizes that he's brought this upon himself by his ridiculous behavior. His parents live in a rural area, twenty minutes out of town, on a "farm." It's not really a farm, of course; at least, it isn't in the sense of a white clapboard house with green shutters and tin basins hung in front for washing. The acreage—they have fifty or so—is all in alfalfa. A neighbor, an actual farmer, keeps it for them. They do have a vintage tractor, which his father plows the long drive with in winter; his mother, in rubber boots and carry-ing a spade, does help with the irrigating from time to time. The house, which they built, is in the Territorial Style, red-tile roofed and adobe walls, which rambles around an interior courtyard planted in succulents. There's a guesthouse, where Andy stays on his visits. The place is airy and comfortable. They have valuable things, of course. When Andy was a child his parents collected paintings and prints. Later it was sculpture, though most of that was sold, and what's left is in the yard around the house, too heavy by far for stealing. Since moving to Zebulon, and even before, his mother had begun with the Indian stuff: Zuni and Zia, San Ildefonso and Second Mesa. Blankets, pots, baskets, hishi, concha and squash-blossom jewelry, kachinas, clay figures, even a medicine man's kit: she has it all. She got started early and certainly now it's worth zillions. More recently, she's turned her eye to "Mexican," by that meaning santos and retablos, death carts and crude paintings on timber of the Virgen de Guadelupe. And everyone knows that it's out there; they throw regular benefits for the chamber festival and the opera and Zebulon College. They don't have any security but for the long drive up the hill, and that is hidden, most of the way in piñon trees. Andy thinks that aspect of it would attract banditos rather than repel them. His mother sees it as a perfect form of "passive" defense. They have argued over this. Her flip remark is "let them take it"; she's tired of the Indian stuff and will give it all later to the library. On the other hand, it may be all a pose: When their mountain house was broken into the winter before, and all that was taken was a guitar and some canned food, she went into such a funk she needed acupuncture.

Andy himself worries a lot about burglars, when he thinks of it. So he is glad to see, despite the suggestion of suspicion that is descending over himself at this particular moment, that the La Queda County emergency people—the police and fire and ambulance drivers—all seem to take their duties very seriously.

"Everything is fine, quite so," he says. "My father's having a little nap—glass of wine at lunch and all that, he's earned it, I guess—and my mother is in town, she keeps a small office there, I'm sure you know that, or at least see the next number there under listings for "Furlong." There aren't any other Furlongs in La Queda County, I'm sure, no nephews or cousins. We're not from here originally, though, now, after twenty years, almost, I'm sure they're well known. I'm visiting from Baltimore, where I live, for a week, a little longer, and everything's fine. It's just that, like an idiot, and I knew it at the time, and see better now for all the trouble that it's causing, I stupidly pushed an unmarked speed-dial button, the first one, I'm a bit bored out here I suppose, and got emergency services. Which I respect, I'm a physician, as I told you. But from not thinking, or thinking rather that it would be less bother just to end it there without bothering you, I hung up."

"Sir, could I have your name?"

"I'm Andy—Dr. Andy, Andrew, rather, Furlong. Of Baltimore. Visiting, as I said. My parents. The Furlongs. Nan and Law. Furlong."

"Mr. *Furlong?* Could you . . . "

"Dr. Furlong, to begin. And it is my name, by the way. I mean, again, I admit fully that I erred in hanging up the telephone without at least notifying you that the call was in error, that there was no emergency at all, not even a problem. Still, I don't see how that small mistake opens me up to charges of lying, which isn't the case, or the disrespect that I'm sensing from you. Ma'am," he adds. The fact of it is that Andy joined his father in a glass or two of wine at lunch; his father has a cellar and drinks out of it. It was a decent bottle with some age on it. They enjoyed it. But he doesn't usually drink at lunch. He doesn't usually drink, period. And, as well, he knows he's a little prone to belligerence when he does. For that reason, and others, he doesn't drink, though he's a physician and knows the purported value of a glass or two of red wine daily.

Just at the moment that he is thinking this, he hears through an open window the unmistakable noise of eight cylinders—eight *American* cylinders, the kind that exist any more only in Impalas or the like—kicking down. He moves to a window where there is a view of the county highway, down the hill, at the edge of the property. It stretches off, like a silver ribbon in the afternoon light, along the mesa and toward town. It looks as if two cruisers, lights flashing but no sirens, are racing in his direction. Like a roadhouse hole-up, he moves to another window, just in time to see the dust rising up in the air from the piñon trees that mask the long drive. It's a state trooper who arrives first, come from the other direction—the barracks that are over by the Indian casinos at Ismay. The big black-and-gold cruiser crunches to a stop in the Furlongs' large graveled drive.

"Okay," he says to the woman, still on the line. Now he under-
stands why she's been circumspect: she's been keeping him on the
phone, as if the true burglar or freight-hopping serial murderer
caught somehow in a grisly double homicide when surprised com-
mitting a botched break-in would linger to chat up emergency services. "The sheriff's here, you've made a terrible mistake, wasting all
sorts of tax dollars." And he hangs up to go talk to the police.

Outside, the trooper hasn't gotten out of his car. He's waiting,
no doubt, for backup. Andy can hear his radio squawking. Shortly,
the two county cars that Andy saw on 650 arrive up the drive as
well, one behind the other. The first parks with the trooper's car
so as to form a wedge. Do they really believe this to be a siege?

Andy thinks that if, somehow, he were able to explain quickly,
his father, who sleeps each afternoon for an hour invariably, might
hear nothing, sleep peacefully, and never find out about the whole
mess. Not that it's anything to be embarrassed over, it's funny really.
However, the sight of police in his driveway brings back one or two
unpleasant associations from his growing-up years that are painful,
frankly, and that he'd prefer entirely not to revisit, especially on this
vacation.

There is a kitchen door, which leads through the succulent garden to a gate in the adobe wall. The police appear focused on the
main gate, which lies around the corner. Andy walks from the side
gate, holding his hands out, striking the kind of grave posture one
picks up in medical school from the senior staff. In his mind, he
halfway expects the trooper and two county police to wheel on
him—he's at their flank—guns weaving in the air and shouting all
kinds of freakish gibberish. Instead, one, the trooper, walks calmly
to him.

"Officer?"

"We got a possible intruder call," he says. "That you?"

"The intruder or the call?" Andy blurts out. Why is he still joking with these people? They plainly don't get it.

"Anyway," the trooper says. He's large, and looks Hispanic,

though he might be Ute Indian, or maybe Navajo, except that Andy read on this visit that the Utes intermarry with Hispanics and the Navajo don't. "We're just checking. Is Law around?"

"Oh," Andy says with relief. His father is gregarious, affable. It doesn't surprise him to find that he might have gotten to know the constabulary. Andy has always been flattered by his father's connections. "You know my father."

"You look like him," says the trooper.

One of the deputies has been listening in. He comes over. "This is Law's son? He's got the same glasses as his dad." Andy's father had made a production, two years before, of ordering frames identical to the ones Andy wears.

"I had them first," Andy says, as he finds himself saying a lot on visits to Zebulon. "Let the record reflect."

"A lawyer, too," the deputy says.

"No, I'm a doctor, actually, as I was telling the dispatcher. A physician. I'm visiting from Baltimore."

"Do you work at John Hopkins?" asks the second deputy.

"I was a resident there, and now I do have an appointment, through, in reality, it's something of a courtesy."

"That's where that sheik went. He died, I think."

"I saw a show about that on the television," the trooper says. "Remember, they gave an x-ray to a whale."

"That was so funny," says the first deputy, the smaller one.

"We're here," the trooper says. "I guess we should say hi. You mind?"

Andy leads them through the red-tiled gallery just inside the front door. Leaving the three of them there, he starts down the long hall at the end of which is his parents' rooms. His knock on the door pushes it open. The bed looks slept upon but is empty. The room has a sliding-glass door that opens onto a small, private courtyard. The curtain dances in the breeze. The courtyard's low wooden gate stands open as well. Out of it, way out at the far corner of the back alfalfa fields, he can see his father with another man.

They appear to be arguing. The other man's hands are flying about, while Andy's father stands by sternly.

Andy walks back to where he has left the trooper and two deputies, not certain what's next. They've seen his father, too, through some living-room windows that look that way. Andy sees them picking single file across the field, boot high in alfalfa and wet with his mother's irrigating.

By the time he catches up with them, there's already a fracas. The neighbor, who is angry about the Furlongs' irrigation for some reason that he can't articulate, has been stealing the alfalfa valves. These head valves are expensive. Law had woken from his nap to see the man, named Ike Service, stealing the third head valve that month. He went out to confront him. When Ike sees the police, he becomes irrational. He lives in a rancher that he built himself, on a quarter acre carved out of the farm next door. He's due only a fraction of the water the Furlongs receive, but he wants to fill a pond. By the time Andy reaches them, they're cuffing him for stealing the valves.

He's cussing a blue streak, talking like a crazy person. The trooper and the two deputies begin leading him back to the house. The field slopes downward and in addition to the main irrigation ditches there are a number of subsidiary tracks, so the ground is very uneven. The soil is adobe, essentially, and his mother has been irrigating. The man is still resisting and jawing and being pushed ahead. He stumbles. The deputy might give him a little extra shove on the way down. It looks to Andy as if the Hispanic or Ute or whatever the state trooper is gives him a jab while he's on the ground with his nightstick.

"Did you see that?" Andy says to his father as they follow behind at a distance.

"You called them, Andy," his father says. "That's what happens when you involve the police in these things."

The deputy and the trooper jerk the man up by his cuffed arms. He looks back to where Andy stands with his father. He has mud and a sprig of alfalfa on his cheek. They lead him around the side of the house. After a moment, Andy and his father hear the doors slam, then see the line of cruisers making their way back down the drive, headed for the county lockup in Bodo Park.

At dinner, over another bottle of remarkable wine, they discuss.

"Why on earth would you call the police?" his mother asks him. "Your father can handle that man."

"I didn't call the police."

"You told me that you did," says his father.

"Now he's going to burn our house down, I'm sure of it."

"Oh, Jesus Christ, Mom."

"I'm serious, he's had two fires over there already."

Andy does remember his mother calling him one day at the hospital to complain that the neighbor, in the midst of an unnecessary home repair, had intentionally set his kitchen on fire for the insurance money. He thinks of his parents, aging and vulnerable, on this isolated quilt-piece of land, miles and miles from anything.

"He probably *will* burn my house down," says Law. "Thanks a lot, Andy. Did you bring this wine?" he asks. "I don't own this."

"I didn't call the police," Andy says.

"My god," says his mother. "Next time say: This is Andy Furlong and everything is fine, thank you, and just hang up. Is that such a task?" she asks. "You dumb cluck."

That night on his way to bed Andy stands for a while in the succulent garden, his head back, looking up at the sky crowded with stars. A light on the northern horizon catches his eye. It is the kitchen window at Ike Service's house, the light going on. He's back. After dinner Law called his friend at the sheriff's and explained. They agreed to just let it go. Now Ike is back in his rancher, the day's experience just another of the resentful memories that crowd his medieval mind. Nan and Law can take care of themselves after all. It is only Andy who reaches out still blindly, in the darkness.

The Thing Itself

When Wallace and Valerie ended their relationship, there was little of the chaos that normally attends such affairs. They had commingled neither property nor obligations. Thirty-six tear-soaked hours *were* spent in an airport hotel at Houston Hobby, no less, when their schedules and the peculiarities of post-9/11 air travel allowed them, after three earlier failed rendezvous, to meet. The proximate cause of their separation, by mutual agreement, was simple. Her position in San Francisco had turned into a quickly climbing and permanent job, one that had the sum of her ambitions neatly inscribed on it. And while Wallace had considered moving to California himself, in the end it was untenable. He was not old enough to cash out, and no longer young enough to cancel the utilities and, with a pink change-of-address card, pull up stakes and go. There was just too much in Baltimore: a web of commercial relations that kept him afloat and two little girls. His business was such a mare's nest of complications that he spoke to his accountant, an obese eccentric who lived and worked in a darkened junior suite of the Carlyle Hotel in Roland Park, four times a week. Sadly, Wallace was neither successful enough to make the move without tolerable consequences nor of so little luck that the occasional sudden migration in pursuit of chimeras of riches or newfound love would be the norm. He was the bourgeoisie, he was the burgher class, new-millennium defined. *It's over,* Wallace said aloud to himself on the day it happened finally, a week still after Houston Hobby, with three telephone calls and two e-mails, each of which informed him, with increasing clarity, that Valerie never wanted to see him again.

There followed five months in his repellent garden apartment with rented furniture. He had a sofa bed, where his daughters slept on alternate weekends. For the first two months, his wife wouldn't speak with him; all their interactions took place through an intermediary, Bliss Perry, a friend from their previous life. In the course of one cold February exchange, Wallace came to learn that Bliss, too, was separated, since Thanksgiving. Hart had left for Cleveland, where he managed one of his company's factories. There wasn't any question about Hart staying in Cleveland—the woman Bliss suspected to exist certainly didn't come from there. After learning this, Wallace began inviting Bliss in on Fridays when she brought his children, with her own three invariably in tow. Wallace looked forward to these visits: They were nearly all the socializing he had. They began to consider sleeping together, and one lovely Friday evening late in March she arrived wearing makeup, a pressed white linen shirt, and tailored slacks in dark gray. Wallace noticed that she even wore the three-quarters parure—a necklace, earrings, and bracelet, all in creamy gold—that Hart had given her after the birth of their third child. He'd never seen her without it before she and Hart separated. Wallace responded to her display with a good bottle of Montrachet, smoked salmon from a package, and an invitation to dinner later in the week. She accepted. However, slick gray days followed, weather retroceding to winter, and her mother-in-law decided against a mid-week drive down from York. Bliss still came to dinner, but with all three girls, their faces dirty and noses running, as well. She was back to wearing jeans and sneakers, topped with baggy layers of sorbet-colored velour and cotton. Neither lipstick nor jewelry was in evidence. The children played with the toys Wallace had collected for his own children in the second bedroom. Bliss and he sat together on the sofa, his arm around her, and watched a movie on television. The unseasonable weather hadn't really mattered: In the end they were both too disconsolate to sleep together. The next Friday it was his wife, Helen, not Bliss, who brought the children, and he never saw Bliss again.

By the beginning of June, with the lease on his garden apartment coming to renewal, Wallace gave his notice. At first he had enjoyed his garden apartment for the stretch of green that rose beyond the large sliding-glass doors and the never-used kitchen. The other units seemed filled with pretty, just-graduated neighbors. They lived in twos and threes all up and down his floor, working at hopeful first jobs in public relations and primary education. Weekends the young women, typically with a silver bolt through their belly buttons or a thorn-rimmed blossom stitched on their ankles, lay beside the complex's pool. Friday nights they dated boys and on Saturday afternoons often brought them there. However, in his depression, he began losing touch with the place, forgetting where he lived when he was away and arriving there later and later each night feeling as if he'd never seen it before. The entire complex, barely two years old and built on a cornfield recently so remote that mice and raccoons still nosed disorientedly about the buildings, already looked worn and shabby. The rental agent was a woman in her thirties who, Wallace imagined, floated like some piscine scavenger snatching with her pointy and small teeth the men who drifted past her on slow downward spirals. She let him know one Sunday (she lived in the complex) that she was available, were he seriously interested. All of it had become too much. Within two weeks of his decision, Helen, who had been bringing the children dutifully each Friday at five and fetching them Sundays by six for two months, invited him to return. The revisit would not be in anyway prodigal. He was to sleep in the first-floor guest room, upon the bed that, despite its clever clothing, sagged to the point of abandon, and the terms of their legal separation would continue to be observed.

For the first week back, Wallace would wake each night to the surprising outline of Helen's sewing machine, on a table by a window, backlit by a waning moon. It had a sinister and hopeless quality. He used the guest bath, compact and pink, with a tiled shower stall and the constant smell of the floral guest soap used in that room alone. Helen never came to his bed and he never went to hers; the children regarded him, or so he thought, from a wary distance. Each morning had a desperate quality to it, and Wallace found himself cowed at the prospect of a confrontation with his wife. His back ached. He began seeing a psychiatrist in Towson. Rightly, she reassured him, he began taking drugs.

The summer melted away, and Wallace, suddenly forty and medicated, spent most late afternoons and weekends in an Adirondack chair wearing nothing but a pair of oil-spotted khaki shorts. He became deeply tanned. He cooked hamburgers and watched his two little girls splash in their blue plastic wading pool. The medicines he used, because there were three, trailed along after them a suite of aftereffects: sweating and chills, frequent spastic yawns, a profound nausea that would sneak up on him like seasickness in the later afternoon. There was a strange twitching in his hands when he felt anxious, accompanied by a general nervousness that made his dreams, when they came, vivid and bizarre. He found himself no happier than he had been before, though his psychiatrist alternately advised him that he *was* better, even if he didn't feel it, and that the entire process was a lengthy one, to which he needed to devote a significant amount of energy and time. From his white Adirondack chair, the slight bowl of his back lawn rising above him, his children barrel rolling with squeals of laughter, and the sun on his chest, the world passed in a constant slow-film blur. The days unfolded insentient to their own order, and time itself had ceased to have character, palpable or kinetic. He woke only with an interest as to when he might sleep again. In the evening he fell asleep with little interest in what sleep would bring.

Salt Lake City's airport lies on the eastern shore of the Great Salt Lake, at the edge of a stream-webbed salt marsh. With the plane's twisting descent, the lake water glinted beneath the sun. Wallace watched as the left wing jiggled first over a large bald island, its face scarred by zigzagging, interlocked trails, then beyond, beneath a regretless August sun, the desert, alkali, ammonia, and pancaked sand.

Wallace and Helen came across his parents immediately in the broad, swept-brick expanse of the resort's lobby. His mother was manipulating, or so it appeared, a concierge, while his father stood at the center of the terra cotta expanse. His masterful stature implied that he waited for something that would never arrive to his perfect satisfaction. One of the strangest aspects of the past two years had been the reinsertion of his parents into the daily mechanics of his life. Like all truly good parents, they had been helpful on the whole, if forever wrong in the fine details. Consequently, Wallace had been required to relearn their personalities, mastering them to a degree he hadn't reached since his teenage years. He wondered sometimes, now that their characters were no longer just a memory, how they had changed in the intervening years, the time in the desert. Not much, he sensed, though he could not be sure.

Out of the lobby's broad windows rose, close enough to touch, the ski mountain, its runs emerald green and smooth looking, separated by membranous stands of roughly sketched Englemann spruce. The place had the sad aura of the entire world in offseason—like a river in drought. The bald banks, the ranks of empty furniture facing the snowless slopes, and the network of slotted metal staircases that invariably ended two steps early all combined to create a singularly charmless scene, a place so forgotten in summer that its future abandonment was all but foreordained.

Helen approached Wallace's mother. They met with a chirp and a hug. Nan, though temperamentally reserved, nevertheless cultivated a lively public persona. Helen, however, had never realized it to be anything other than her mother-in-law's natural self. Wallace met his father in the center of the naked expanse. The breaks on his mother's car had failed on the drive to Salt Lake from Zebulon.

"And your mother carries a second set of license plates in the trunk of the Jag," he said to his son.

"What happened?" Wallace made a mental note to ask his mother about the second set of plates later.

"She claims she had it checked before we drove out. I blame Roy. He's an idiot. I don't know why your mother insists on taking her car to him. In Deschene I realized that we had no breaks. Glided to a stop at the first filling station we came to in Salt Lake."

"Honestly, you had no brakes?"

"We had underperforming brakes."

"Where are Andy and Kim?"

"At her parents' house. Tying bird seed and jelly beans into organza." Wallace's younger brother was getting married finally, to a postdoc in public hygiene. Her name was Kim Birdsall, and she did research on prophylactic contraception, specifically, a clear ooze that increased the acidity of a woman's vagina. Kim had assured him the first time they met that it was actually quite messy. What Andy saw in her, especially given the parade of pin-ups he'd dated vigorously over the past five years, Wallace did not know. Certainly Kim was nice, serious, and well-meaning; however, she left everyone, especially the brother's parents, perplexed. She was small and plain, and wore her public hygiene earnestness like a photo ID clipped to the white lapel flapping over her flat chest. Even at this moment, Wallace could sense his father, watching Helen closely, and wondering, Wallace supposed, how affairs could have come to this. Early on, Law had said to both his sons—*Jesus Christ, you guys, marry for money. That's what I did. How do you think I have any?* First Wallace married Helen, and now Andy was marrying for love alone.

Wallace kissed his mother and excused himself to check in.

"I've done it," Nan said. She opened her handbag and produced the key envelope. Law now joined them.

"We looked at them both," he said. "And took the nicer of the two." Tall and slim still, Wallace's father wore a white shirt, a seersucker jacket, and a tie.

"We're going into town to help Nettie Birdsall with the favors and table ornaments," Nan said.

"Dad is?"

"Law is going to a bookstore," Nan said. "And he wants to see Joseph Smith."

She meant the statue.

Later that afternoon, Nan and Law, Wallace and Helen, and Andy found themselves at a taco restaurant in the Wasatch foothills. One of Andy's roommates from medical school owned it. He had dropped out after two years, and now he owned a chain of taco restaurants, stretching from Provo to Ogden. Nan and Law had taken an interest in him, Thatcher Harris, early on. Now, by the way he was giving them the tour, Wallace realized that they had invested in him. Wallace easily understood the attraction—he was a handsome man, tall and fit, with sandy hair that tended toward red in sunlight. He'd been smart enough to be admitted to Stanford Med, and smarter still, according to Andy, to get out when he could. He had a winning way to him, Wallace recognized, even if his quick charm, regardless of how often deployed, never seemed to result in any lasting sort of acquaintance. Even Andy over the years had felt jilted by him, ostensibly one of his closest friends.

And yet here he was, leading the band of Furlongs through his store, proudly pointing out the glistening stainless commercial appliances, the walk-in refrigerator, the inventive steam table of his own design. Only Helen had never met Thatcher before. Wallace could tell that she was taken by him. He was the sort of guy her eye had always been drawn to, since they first began dating. Previously, he wrote his wife's attractions off as frivolous—*relationships with pretty boys never last,* she had once told him years before, in a moment of uncommon openness. However, they never failed to pocket her attention. Now she followed him at the head of the pack, laughing at each of his jokes and tipping her head down whenever he matched her gaze.

Wallace and Andy pulled up the rear. Seeing his wife's flirtations caused him not jealousy but only to think of Valerie and sentenced him to yet another totally disconsolate mood.

By the time they had each eaten a *tacquito,* drunk a pony Corona, and climbed into the large, rented SUV, it had become clear to Wallace that his wife had said something to Thatcher, at the very least, if they hadn't already made some sort of plan. She sat silent, staring distantly at the mountains that passed on the steep, quick ascent to Snowbird. Wallace watched the shadows move alternately with strong, late-afternoon sun across her sharp face.

Andy narrated as he drove. He would drop them at the resort, giving them just barely enough time to change for the rehearsal and make it back down through the canyon to the church. The clouds, already clotting up, would produce the usual late showers, thus ruining the terrace cocktails before dinner that Nan and Nettie Birdsall had planned following the rehearsal. In the meantime, he would rush to the flower mart to pick up an order for Mrs. Birdsall, which might have been delivered if she had not been so confident that such an important task would best be handled by her future son-in-law one half-hour before his wedding rehearsal.

Grumbling still, Andy kicked them all out of his vehicle at the resort's strange underground entrance (another allusion, Wallace assumed, to the season it was not) and sped away in his huge, groaning truck.

As they drove down the valley, it began to rain. By the time the short rehearsal was completed, the storm had blown away, though the roads and sidewalks still glistened. They were early, among the first to arrive at the restaurant. Wallace helped his mother with the final preparations: more wine, sparkling water for every table, a re-arrangement of the flowers that Andy had delivered earlier in the afternoon.

The guests began coming. By chance, though in different places, Wallace and Helen both noticed when Thatch Harris entered the room. Helen's eyes lit up. She smiled in a way Wallace himself thought that he'd never seen her smile.

Kim Birdsall's Canadian relatives arrived, her mother's brothers, cousins, nieces, and nephews. The room got crowded. Dinner was served; dinner was finished. When he looked for Helen, he usually found her near Thatcher. During the dessert and coffee, he noticed, she made a concerted effort to sit with Nettie Birdsall and her women relatives. But Thatch Harris hovered nearby, glancing at her often with appreciative affection. Had Wallace himself not felt so completely wounded already, he would have felt greater wounding still. As it was he could only look on with dumb recognition. Had he ever been so obvious in his own dalliances?

Following the dinner, everyone but Kim, her sister, and her parents, who were spending the night at the Birdsall's house, returned in a caravan of sorts up the mountain. In the parking garage, the men agreed to meet at a bar in the resort's village, someplace they'd heard live music coming from the night before. After parting wordlessly with Helen in the lobby, Wallace walked down to the tavern where the menfolk were gathering. At the bar, he was confronted with a tired-looking bartender, her blonde hair pulled back tight and falling down her back in a loose ponytail.

"Is there someone who could be my sponsor?" he asked her.

"Rick will be your sponsor this evening," she said, looking past him at no one in particular.

Andy was at the center of a gathering of tables and chairs. One part of the symphony was made of Kim's relatives. Another large section was composed of the groomsmen friends of Andy's whom Wallace recognized from photographs or skiing trips over the years. Thatcher Harris was, of course, missing. Besides Law, who still dressed in a seersucker jacket and bow tie, Wallace was Andy's only relative there. The Furlongs came from a large family to which nobody had spoken in decades.

Law left first, after drinking a Scotch. Wallace had another beer, though he wasn't much interested in drinking. His psychiatrist discouraged it, and Helen blamed his lapses of memory—those events that disappeared regularly into the void of his palliated identity—on wine. He didn't know.

When Andy's part of the group decided to drive back down the mountain in search of naked dancing, Wallace took his leave. He climbed the dark asphalt trail that wound back up to the mass of the resort's main buildings. The resort's blank western face had been embedded with strange organic shapes, which formed the grips and holds of a climbing wall. Though it was late, the swimming pool's rubbery light still reflected off the wall's lower stories, accompanied by suggestive feminine laughter. Only a small strip of night sky, choked with anonymous stars, was visible above.

Helen was not in the room. Wallace fell asleep watching a late movie on the television. It was something about three roommates who genetically recombined one of their professors to be the man of each of their dreams. Even in soft-core porn, however, such a plan was doomed to go afoul. Not even the creature's robotic sex and heightened sense of domestic tidiness could compare with the hurly-burly of normal love.

Helen returned to the room at 3:30 in the morning, according to the dully glowing clock radio. She undressed by the bathroom light, removed her contacts, washed her face, and crawled into in the other bed.

Kim Birdsall's parents were Catholics of an eastern sort, which celebrated its religious holidays with all sorts of Cyrillic festoons and inflections. Andy was required to wear a towering, fez-shaped hat, a bracelet of coins, and have his shoulders tapped with a loaf of salt bread. Before the ceremony, Wallace stood by his brother in the

vestry with the priest, who was most definitely not of this cultic per-
suasion and regarded it dryly, awaiting the organist's cue. When it
came, Wallace accompanied his brother along the whispering aisle.
Nettie and André Birdsall, with the assistance of two of Nettie's
brothers, performed the ritual of the salt bread. Helen helped co-
ordinate the tossing of the birdseed when Andy and his wife
emerged from the church.

The reception was held at the resort. Wallace and Helen rode
with Nan and Law in Andy's rented SUV. Kim had hired a limou-
sine for her and Andy's drive. After the meal, André gave a toast,
as did Law, then Wallace. There was a dance, first with just Andy
and Kim, followed by each of the groomsmen, paired with a bridesmaid.

Thatcher Harris, who, like Wallace, had worn a black tuxedo
and stood beside Wallace at the alter and in the photographs, remained cheerful, helpful, and cooperative. An old girlfriend, now
living in Big Piney, Wyoming, was his date. She drank too much,
while Thatcher, who looked slimmer, more tanned, and more beautiful than any of the groomsmen, or the groom, even, flirted with
a bridesmaid. Helen played her part, or the lack thereof—as the
wife of a groomsman, as a sister-in-law of the greatest remove—
with little enthusiasm. She sat with Nan and Law at their table (because the wedding party sat at the head of the room, as if they were
a panel of assembled experts) and left immediately after the toasts.

The hours melted away insensibly. Dusk came over the eastern peaks and the Englemann spruce trees resumed their shadowy
sentry. There was dancing and the usual hijinks.

When the evening was just Andy and Kim and their friends, sitting again at the center of attention, and the groomsmen had
helped Nettie Birdsall carry the ceremonial breads and leftover organza party favors to her car in the underground garage, Wallace
looked briefly for Helen. Neither she—nor Thatcher Harris, for
that matter—was anywhere to be found. Wallace rode the elevator
to his floor, to the room his mother had bought for him. He had

forgotten to ask her about the second set of license tags in the trunk of her Jag. Now that he'd remembered the mystery again, he knew that he would forget it forever. The tags would slip into the great green void of those things between them which were never spoken of. He inserted the card key into the door until the signal light fluttered. It struck him how much was expected of that tiny light, smaller than a pencil's eraser. With a downward click he opened the door. Helen was there, sitting in a chair in the dark, the only light in the room reflected from the swimming pool below. She had changed into jeans, a camisole, and a pile shirt. Her bare heels rested on the seat and she hugged her knees to her chest. She smelled of cigarette smoke.

Wallace walked past her and out onto the balcony. The pool lay below, in a steady marine glow. Two young couples, guests from the wedding Wallace guessed by their dress, sat talking at a table near the water. He heard a laugh, and then the ring of a chair being moved against the pavement. The breeze came up and it riffled the water, causing chaos among the shadows. Wallace turned and looked to Helen, where she sat tightly balled in the chair. The reflected light licked at her bare feet. He thought it was like—but it was like nothing. The moment was unique. It resembled nothing; it was the thing itself.

Louis Rosenstock © 2003

Tristan Davies is Senior Lecturer and Director of Undergraduate Studies at The Writing Seminars at Johns Hopkins University. In 2001, he received the Excellence in Teaching Award from the Johns Hopkins Alumni Association. His stories have appeared in the journals *Glimmer Train*, *Boulevard*, *The Mississippi Review*, *The Columbia Review*, *Snowflake*, and *Sundog*.

The stories collected in *Cake*, his first book, move fluidly between styles. The longer stories capture a psychologically complex realism while the shorter pieces forego the conventions of the contemporary short story in favor of incantatory lyricism. The oldest story in this collection, "Talent Show," was written early in 1997. The stories "Dan, Astrid Says," and "The Thing Itself" were finished last, in the autumn of 2002. "Andromeda," "Night," "Cake," and some of the other short pieces were originally written together and conceived of as a single piece. "Counterfactuals" is the vestigial remnant of a mid-length novel. "In the Woodlands" is based on an actual couple killed by police in a shoot-out on May 7, 1995, following a high-speed chase that ended in the median of Interstate 26 near Charleston, South Carolina. Solitude, referred to at the end of "Personals," is a house built in 1784 by John Penn, Jr., a grandson of William Penn. He abandoned his house and the country in 1788 upon learning that the new republic had no intention of honoring his family's claims. The house and grounds, which overlook the Schuylkill, are now part of the Philadelphia Zoo.

Fiction Titles in the Series

Guy Davenport, *Da Vinci's Bicycle*
Stephen Dixon, *14 Stories*
Jack Matthews, *Dubious Persuasions*
Guy Davenport, *Tatlin!*
Joe Ashby Porter, *The Kentucky Stories*
Stephen Dixon, *Time to Go*
Jack Matthews, *Crazy Women*
Jean McGarry, *Airs of Providence*
Jack Matthews, *Ghostly Populations*
Jean McGarry, *The Very Rich Hours*
Steve Barthelme, *And He Tells the Little Horse the Whole Story*
Michael Martone, *Safety Patrol*
Jerry Klinkowitz, *"Short Season" and Other Stories*
James Boylan, *Remind Me to Murder You Later*
Frances Sherwood, *Everything You've Heard Is True*
Stephen Dixon, *All Gone*
Jack Matthews, *Dirty Tricks*
Joe Ashby Porter, *Lithuania*
Robert Nichols, *In the Air*
Ellen Akins, *World Like a Knife*
Greg Johnson, *A Friendly Deceit*
Guy Davenport, *The Jules Verne Steam Balloon*
Guy Davenport, *Eclogues*
Jack Matthews, *"Storyhood As We Know It" and Other Tales*
Stepen Dixon, *Long Made Short*
Jean McGarry, *Home at Last*
Jerry Klinkowitz, *Basepaths*
Greg Johnson, *I Am Dangerous*
Josephine Jacobsen, *What Goes without Saying*
Jean McGarry, *Gallagher's Travels*
Richard Burgin, *Fear of Blue Skies*
Avery Chenoweth, *Wingtips*
Judith Grossman, *How Aliens Think*
Glenn Blake, *Drowned Moon*
Robley Wilson, *The Book of Lost Fathers*
Richard Burgin, *The Spirit Returns*
Jean McGarry, *Dream Date*